Naked came the farmer

A Round-Robin Rural Romance and Murder Mystery

By Philip Jose Farmer, Bill Knight, David Everson,
Jerry Klein, Julie Kistler, Nancy Atherton,
Steven Burgauer, Joel Steinfeldt, Joseph Flynn,
Terry Bibo, Garry Moore, Tracy Knight and Dorothy Cannell

Mayfly
Elmwood, Illinois

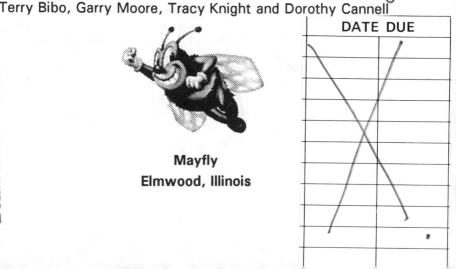

NAKED CAME THE FARMER

Mayfly Productions
P.O. Box 380
Elmwood, IL 61529-0380

The chapters in this book were originally serialized in the *Daily Times* (Pekin, Ill.) and in the Community Service Newspapers chain of weeklies (Peoria, Ill.)

Library of Congress Catalog Card Number: 98-65072
ISBN: 0-9624613-7-7

Cover by Roland Millington/Accuprint (Pekin, Ill.)
Graphics assistance from Sharon Williams/*The Labor Paper* (Peoria, Ill.)

Printed in the United States of America
Versa Press (East Peoria, Ill.)

Profits from the sale of this book go to Friends of the Peoria Public Library, Inc.

Dedicated to Readers

Contents

"My main trouble was that I had no sense of humor."

--Frankenstein's Monster

"Up the jungle-bound Congo River of 1890 on a steamboat in Conrad's "Heart of Darkness?"? No more savage or scary than in a canoe up the Kickapoo Creek in 1990.

--Peoria As Will and Idea, M. Corbie

Chisholm's Law: Any time things seem to be getting better, you have overlooked something.

1
NAKED CAME
THE FARMER

Philip Jose Farmer

The freight train, a quarter of a mile east from the back of Cassie's farmhouse, rumbled loudly. Its bass horn blasted again and again as it neared the junction of two county roads. She glanced at her wristwatch. It was 9:10 of a beautiful though cloudy night in rural Tazewell County, Illinois. October 31, Halloween, was only five days away.

She resumed reading The Book of Job. The once-rich and happy Job has just lost all of his many herds and herdsmen. Now, the last of the messengers tells him a whirlwind has killed all his children. Job tears off his cloak, shaves his head, falls on the ground, and cries, "Naked came I from the womb! Naked I shall return from where I came!"

Without warning, a roar as if made by Job's whirlwind itself struck Cassie's house. The floor shook. The TV set danced and almost tipped over. Glass broke upstairs. She reared out of the chair, the Bible falling from her lap.

The roar passed on, and the house quit trembling. Something banged loudly on the floor above. Something rolled down the stairway from upstairs. It was as large and as round as... oh, no! No! No!

It bumped down the steps and bounced onto the floor. It rolled across the polished hardwood floor, slowed down, and stopped a few feet to her right. One of its eyes was open, and it was looking up at her. The other hung out of the hole in the socket from the end of the optic nerve.

Large and round as a head.

She found it hard not to scream. But she didn't.

The head was a man's. Though battered and beaten, it was a head she knew well. Even if it had been faceless, the taped and bandaged nose would have told her who it was. She'd seen its owner only a week ago at the special county board meeting in Pekin. Subject: the mega-hog farm and waste lagoon a mile from her property. The stink of excrement from 30,000 pigs was bad enough in the fall. But in summer...!

Last week, at the protest meeting, her fingers had closed around the neck of Ron Rassendeal, manager of the Porklips Now, Inc. farm. Yet, two months ago, they'd fallen deeply in love after they met in his Bible class in the Church of the Deferred Judgment. They were to be married in Pawsitee, their native village. But when he became the manager of the mega-hog farm, she handed the betrothal ring back to him. Until the demonstration, they'd not spoken to each other.

However, during the meeting, Ron Rassendeal had insulted her again and again. Justifiably enraged, she'd said she'd rather mate with the Creature From The Waste Lagoon than with him, a traitor to his own people. He retorted that Cassie had no business being a private investigator. That was a man's work. Then he commented most bitingly on the fact that, though 31, she was still unmarried, probably because she was so very skinny. He ended by loudly saying: "You look like seven years of the famine in Egypt. Like the afterbirth of the Apocalypse."

That made her see red and a few other colors. For most of her life, she'd been mocked because she was obese. Now, after years of suffering in dieter's hell, to be insulted because she was too thin! Too much!

She didn't remember breaking his nose with the bottom of a water pitcher she'd grabbed from the desk. She did remember squeezing his neck. The minister of their church, the Rev. Rice Roylott, had pulled her off the bleeding man. And then, red-faced, bellowing, he'd punched Rassendeal in his belly. So that made two who'd just committed one of the seven deadly sins: anger.

She was not surprised at such violent conduct from such a churchly man. For a long time, she'd suspected that the good-looking reverend secretly loved her. She supposed it was because she looked so much like his beloved uncle. Whatever, he couldn't say anything to her about his concealed desire until after his alcoholic wife died of cirrhosis of the liver. Which she was close to doing.

Cassie was out on bail now, awaiting trial for aggravated assault and battery, among other things. She thought, though, that Rassendeal might drop the charges. He was six feet three inches tall and weighed 230 pounds. He'd lost a lot of face by pressing charges against a woman five feet six inches tall and weighing 90 pounds.

Cassie thought, It's too late now for him to back out. He's permanently lost face.

She giggled, couldn't help it, gruesome as the thought was. But it booted her out of her paralysis. She stepped around the head, went to the phone, and, her voice close to quavering, called the county sheriff's department.

Sgt. Carl Lynn answered.

9

She said, "It's Cassie Canine." She pronounced it KuhNINE, not KAY-nine, thank you.

After she'd told him what had happened, he said, "Get out of the house now. Drive to the state road. Stay parked there with your doors locked until we show up."

That was good advice, but she wasn't taking it. Whatever had caused the roaring, the house shaking, and the glass breaking, it had been outside of the house. And that head, she was sure, hadn't propelled itself through the window.

Close to the bottom of the steps, she saw a fragment of what had to be from a pumpkin. As she climbed higher, she came across more pieces of a shattered pumpkin. Obviously, they had been broken off when the head, encased in the pumpkin, had hit the bedroom floor.

The many yellow and curving pieces scattered over the hardwood floor confirmed her surmise. Some pieces glued together, part of the original encasement of the head, doubly confirmed it. She didn't touch these. Her P.I. training had taught her not to mess with the evidence.

She looked out of the window. Several Klieg lights illuminated the stretch of soil, its soybean crop now harvested. The gravel country road just beyond it and the O.P.U. railroad tracks just past the road were bare of life. The legend-haunted Indian mound in the corner of the field was a dim figure. The ghosts of those buried within it long before the Pawsitee Indians settled here were supposed to come out on Halloween eve. But why should they? Halloween would mean nothing to them.

She went downstairs and out onto the well-lighted front porch and front yard. Near the entrance to the gravel driveway was a huge FOR SALE sign. Her now-dead father had put it up as soon as Porklips Now, Inc. had won the legal right to build the mega-hog farm. But who'd buy land that was an abomination in the nostrils of the Lord and of His creatures, too? However, to ensure that his daughter would continue the fight against Porklips Now, Inc., Mr. Canine had willed Cassie the farm provided she lived in it.

The paved two-lane state road just outside the western fence of the farm ran past the mega-hog farm, which was a half-mile west of it. The traffic of lights from cars and trucks looked normal for this time of evening. And then she saw, far down the road and coming fast, the flashing lights of the first of the county sheriff's vehicles.

She stepped back out to greet the officers. The county coroner arrived a few minutes after the police. For an hour there was a lot of noise and of her telling what had happened. There was much questioning, flashing of camera lights, measuring with tape, chalking of the floors, shaking of heads, and puzzled looks. The deputies also examined the premises around the house and the gravel road.

Sgt. Lynn said, "There's no way Rassendeal's head could've been thrown from the road. What could do that? Even if something could do it from half a mile away, it couldn't be accurate enough to go through the window."

"You're not thinking, Carl," she said. "How about the Aludium Q36 Pumpkin Modulator?"

The sergeant slapped his forehead. "Only 40 and getting senile! Well, maybe! Morning comes, I'll call Matt Parker, tell him to find out if the modulator's been stolen or looks like maybe it had been. I doubt it very very much, but I can't ignore anything."

Cassie also doubted it, and she knew the sergeant had to investigate her story of tonight's events, too. He would be thinking that she could have thrown the head through the window from outside the house while standing on a ladder. Then she could have set up things to look as if the pumpkin had shattered on striking the bedroom floor.

At long last, the head was put in a box, the fragments were collected, and everything the men thought should be done was done. As soon as the last car pulled away, Cassie put the coffee cups and the doughnut and cookie plates into the dishwasher. Then she called her partner in Peoria. But she had to leave messages at his house and at the offices of Canine and Pavlow, Private Investigators.

After this, she phoned her lawyer in Morton, chiefly known as the Pumpkin Capital of the world. Alaric Ostrogoth, a junior partner in the steamroller firm of Hyksos, Goldinhord, and Asshur, was not home. She left a message telling him she might be a suspect in the murder of Ron Rassendeal. She was innocent, but this case was so bizarre!

She had no sooner hung up than the phone rang again. The call was from Sam Sheafhecker, one of her temporarily hired observers. He lived near Mackinaw, a small town southeast of Morton.

"Hey, Miss Canine! I seen her! I seen her! She went by like a flash of light not five feet from where I was! I was just about to cross Route 9 when... zoom! She was come and gone, but I saw her in all her shameful glory! The White White Witch herself! But she ain't scheduled to show tonight! Halloween's five days away! How you figure that?"

Cassie told Sam to calm down and report as she'd trained him to do. After a struggle, he did so. The woman on the big black Harley-Davidson, its headlight off, had sped past him at 11:32 p.m. The lights from a nearby gas station had illuminated her fully though briefly. Sam had called her the White White Witch, a favorite term of the journalists. Some referred to her as the Venus de Motorcycle; others, as the Blond Pimpernel. Eyewitnesses described her as statuesque, Junoesque, and wow!

For four years, starting with the night of April Fool's Day, she had shot out of the darkness and back into it down backcountry roads, county roads, and even state highways. She also appeared, always between the hours of 11:30 p.m. and 12:30 a.m., on Maypole Day, July 4th, Lincoln's Birthday, Labor Day, and Halloween. From leather bags on the sides of her machine, she pulled out leaflets and scattered them behind her. These were blank except for one word: REVENGE!

The police of three counties were on the lookout for her. But, though she'd narrowly escaped being caught a dozen times, she was still showing up in her costume or, rather, lack of it. Where she'd pop out, no one could predict.

Cassie was amused rather than outraged by the woman. And she admired her, though she didn't really know why. What was the woman up to? Why were the leaflets so enigmatic? And now, since the cops had failed to arrest her, a council of indignant citizens had hired Cassie to catch the woman. The Rev. Roylott, the council head, had asked Cassie to be the chief investigator and at much less than her accustomed fee. She'd agreed, reluctantly, to accept the case.

After she'd quit questioning Sheafhecker, she went upstairs and stuffed rags under the closed door of the bedroom to keep the October night chill away from the rest of the house. She didn't fancy sleeping in the same room or even on the same story where her ex-fiance's severed head had been, however briefly. Tomorrow, she'd install a new window and clean everything up. Then she headed downstairs. There, she got out sheets, a blanket, and pillows and arranged them on the living room couch. After she was washed and pajamaed, she set the security alarm and got under the covers.

At four in the morning, she was still awake. Many questions about that hideous crime and visions of the head kept knocking like trick-or-treaters on the door of her mind. Also, very vivid memories rose up from the center of her being, images of humiliating scenes when she had been mocked because she was so obese. Not until she enrolled in Oral Roberts University was she spared these. It was during her four years there that she cast out the twin sins of gluttony and anger, shed 150 pounds, and only rarely lost her temper. Well, maybe it was more often than rarely.

She graduated magna cum laude, her major being Criminology and her minor being Theology. After all, the two were allied, both dealing with sinners and evil-doers. She also won first place in a much-publicized intercollegiate debate. Subject: When Adam caught his first cold, from whom did he catch it? She was interested in all kinds of mysteries, not just those concerned with law-breaking.

After graduation, she'd fallen from grace. The Rev. Roylott had brought her back to a state of unfallenness. But his church insisted that its members' Biblical literalism be seen through a glass, metaphysically. ...

She must have gone to sleep. The ringing of the doorbell shot her up out of the bedclothes like Jonah spit out by the big fish. She took out the .38 six-shooter revolver from under the pillow next to hers. Then she looked through the front door peephole. The front porch and the yard beyond it were brightly lit. Nobody there. After lifting the blinds all along the room and seeing nothing alarming, she went back to the peephole. She'd wait one minute, then she'd call the county police. What had happened tonight had made her very nervous.

Suddenly, a head appeared. But, unlike the previous one she'd encountered, it was attached to the neck, which rose from broad white shoulders. Its owner had been hiding by the front of the high porch. She waited. A minute passed or perhaps it was two or three minutes. Then the body appeared at the foot of the steps. All of the man, all of which was unclothed, came up the steps to the front porch. The man rang the doorbell, then turned in a flash of flesh and was again concealed by the high rise of the porch.

Whatever the reason for his being here, his identity was no mystery. He was Rudy Rassendeal, Ron's brother. Thirty-eight years old, tall, well-built, handsome, rich, and cunning in money matters but otherwise stupid. A great catch. He owned the Pronobis Used Car Agency in Pawsitee. COME ONE! COME ALL!! GET A REAL RASSENDEAL!!! She loathed him because he'd cheated Cassie's father-- and many others-- on a deal.

Worse than that, Rassendeal fervently supported a state legislator, Mortimer Mux, Major Moron. Mux was a do-nothing politician. But, now and then, the big corporation lobbyists, Satanic sorcerers all, used their unholy incantations to call him up from the deepest deep and the vastest vastness of his corpsish coma to do their evil will. That done, he quit haunting the halls and stalls of Springfield, the state capital, and sank back into the extreme lassitude of Dracula during daylight.

It was Mux who had rammed through the state legislature the laws permitting the mega-hog farm to be built near Pawsitee. That he had been re-elected twice indicated to Cassie that too many voters in the county couldn't or didn't read the newspapers. Or perhaps it was true that the ozone hole was somehow causing a steep drop in the average I.Q.

Cassie turned the security system off and unlocked the front door. Holding her revolver, she stepped out onto the porch.

"Rudy Rassendeal! I know you're down there. What in Sam Hill are you doing here?"

Rassendeal said, "Give me a blanket, and then I'll come in. I know you hate me, but I don't mean no harm. Can't you hear my teeth chattering? Let me in so I can get warm. Then I'll tell you what happened to me, though I ain't sure you'll believe it. I don't hardly believe it myself. Then you can notify the sheriff if you think you should."

Cassie went back into the house and took her blanket from the couch.

She thought, If he's got a story, it must be a doozy.

2
SEEING RED

Bill Knight

Morning's twilight sky was slate gray, except for a white sliver at the horizon. From the west, a storm was sweeping through the Midwest with the lazy pace of an old-time prairie fire, relentless and merciless. The dirt lane from the gravel township road already was littered with burnt-red leaves blown from the old oaks along the way. A few bare branches had fallen from the elegant stand of ancient elms that somehow had survived decades of disease and death to form a protective canopy between the house and barn. Beneath the shady elms was a well-worn path where proof of a privy and a pumphouse remained if people looked.

But no one looked. Red lived alone.

The oaks and elms, the maples and apple orchard, even the hackberry and mulberry junk trees all alternated between stillness and frenzy, as gusts ahead of the advancing cold front occasionally whipped their branches. The rusted tin roof on the machine shed shook. Then the rising sun flared over Earth's edge. Above the fields but below the cloud bank, sunrise glowed gold like a kitchen match lowered to a lamp.

"Gotta hurry," Red Pavlow huffed, hustling toward the slag heap, erupting harsh and pink like a boil in the bean field, some

100 yards south. "A little late."

Red's combine was still hot from finishing his beans before the frost forecast for tonight. He'd taken advantage of a warm wind and worked the rest of the night after doing corn late at Cassie's. Although he worked with Cassie as her partner-- bird-dogging for attorneys, insurance companies, even an occasional divorce client-- he also worked for her on the farm. "Detective dirt farmer," he thought aloud: "This gun for hire/hired hand."

A series of protests about PNI's planned land grabs delayed picking. Now Red was caught up, almost. Just a few loose ends. He figured he'd grab a nap and shower and get to Canine & Pavlow's Peoria office by 9. It was going to be a busy day. But first, he needed his daily witness. Prayer time. Being here, he thought.

Binoculars hung from Red's neck, clacking against the buttons on his bib overalls. Reaching the base of the slag heap, he doffed his cloth Cubs cap and ran his hand through his close-cropped, ink-black hair. He inhaled deeply, his high cheekbones and hawk nose wrinkling with a slight smile. The air was warm, weighted with moisture. But it never lost its odors-- some delicate and aromatic, others foul and vile.

There was the smell of the soil, of course, plus traces of fallen leaves and apples, and scents from the lavender and mint by the porch. And sometimes, when a careless breeze blew, there was the mega-farm a few miles away, where 30,000 hogs were born or bred, weaned or fed, slaughtered or packaged-- all while leaving behind, in open pits and storage tanks, the equivalent of a city of 60,000 in urine, manure and germs.

"Crap," Red said, his work boots sliding a few inches down the slope as he climbed. His eyes watered with wind from the cesspool the company called a lagoon. The smell could choke people with a grip, deep in throats. He wiped his face on his shirt sleeve and resumed moving up the incline.

The pile of red rock was left over from a mine that had flourished decades ago, gouging up the earth right to the property line, stripping off layers of coal, starting with the topsoil and finishing with reclaimed acreage pocked with pits and these occasional mini-mountains. Red's dad had been a miner at Rapatee, driving from Red's mother's home near Maquon in Knox County.

Now, they were all gone-- his family, their homeplace. In the meantime, the hardscrabble strip-mine land became gentle meadows, mostly treeless rolling humps-- a soulless South Dakota. But here and there, on the ridges between deep trenches tearing through the country, were trees and brush and ponds once stocked with bass.

Reaching a ledge near the slag heap's summit 100 feet above the fields, Red watched and waited... maybe for a sun dog mirrored in the clouds, a hawk hunting, ground fog, pole lights blinking off, a pheasant. Birds chirped. Red sighed with love and fear.

He used to see hummingbirds here, he thought. No more. Fewer finches, too. And frogs. Fish seemed doomed to float with open sores and dead eyes downstream from Porklips Now's Factory Farm 5, one of 15 farrowing, nursery or finishing operations between Bloomington and Burlington. Even geese flying through the area, seeking open water, avoided the lagoons.

"Like the plague," Red murmured, scowling.

Here on the heap, sunrise came a few seconds earlier, sunset later. He liked the light, but the night also had charms.

He thought the best witnessing may be around midnight for meteors: white streaks turned gold-green, burning minerals. He understood how his ancestors, the Potawatomie, living in villages near here, would pray and dance and sing when such strange, celestial things happened. Scanning the sky and land, Red felt part of the landscape: natural. Threatened. He needed Divine intervention.

"Great Father?" he asked aloud, but didn't know what to say next. So he waited for the clouds to shift, the sky to change. From his niche carved in the slag heap, Red could look for miles in three directions, above trees, past a neighbor's round barn to an old concrete silo, at former farms' decrepit windmills, toward the village's water tower or the glass-and-metal skyline of Peoria. Standing, he could look in the other direction and see through the brackish smog and clouds of flies above PNI's mega-farm cesspools.

On some muggy summer nights, yellow sodium-vapor lights at Canton and Galesburg prisons reflected off clouds, he thought, wondering where Kewanee's new prison would show. In the winter, Red sometimes climbed up on crisp, raw days to watch steam clouds belch from the smokestacks in Havana, Canton, Bartonville and Pekin.

He heard the cry of a crow, and became aware of a gravel dust cloud coming south on the township road, rocks pinging off its undercarriage occasionally heard above the roar of the engine.

"Hmph," Red said. "Cops?"

●

"Are you trying to blackmail me, Rudy?"

Cassie had had about enough from the surviving Rassendeal. After she'd opened her door, the naked brother of her late former fiance had retrieved a taped shoe box from the yard by the porch steps and approached her door before the stink struck her like a shock wave. She almost vomited.

Retreating inside, she grabbed a blanket from the couch for Rudy to cover himself, held her nose and shooed him to the shower upstairs. Bits of brown, dried leaves and weeds fell from Rudy as he went. Back now, dressed in Cassie's sweatsuit, he said he'd discarded his clothes after being tossed into the Tazewell megafarm's lagoon. He said her pastor or partner might be involved.

"All I know is, I parked at the church lot to ask your hired hand about buying his truck, that nice old Chevy," Rudy continued. "I waved him down from your combine and he came over and we talked. He got mad. He called me names, lifted my car hood, ripped out the spark-plug wires and kicked my butt."

"He assaulted you?"

"No, he... well, he kicked me-- in the pants. Then he walked away, climbed into the combine cab, and started harvesting again."

"What's that got to do with you stewing in your own juices?"

"All I know is, I couldn't get in the church to use the phone -- it was locked-- and started walking down the road to call somebody when I remembered my box. I didn't want to leave it, so I went back to get it from the car. That's when it happened."

"You were thrown into the cesspool."

"Right. Lifted up and tossed in the lagoon like a bag of trash. I tried to get out-- I did get out-- but it was so slippery and smelly and muddy that I kept falling. Finally, I managed to crawl out, coughing, puking. And I just passed out. When I came to I had to peel off my clothes before I passed out again."

"So much for PNI brochures. What do they call manure? 'Benign nutrients'?" Cassie asked. "What's all this got to do with Red?"

"All I know is, he got mad. And the only other car around was Pastor Rice's, at the church. Like I say, I suppose it could've been the preacher, too."

Rudy looked around the living room. His toes tapped, his mouth twitched and he kept licking his lips. He still smelled.

"Where'd you hear about Ron?"

"Um. You know. The radio."

Cassie thought of incessant campaign commercials for the upcoming elections and looked at her wristwatch. It was 6:45 a.m. "Again, Rudy, you're making this late-night dip my problem? You're threatening to go to the police unless... unless what? Call the cops, that's fine. Let's see where this all falls."

"Have the police questioned you yet?"

"About Ron? Sure, they were here. Why?"

"All I know is, I almost bought the farm tonight-- "

"Well, now, that's part of the problem, isn't it, Rudy? PNI wants to expand again and you and your brother are leading the way? Or, were. Isn't that the problem?"

"Well, no. At least, not all of it."

•

Riding down the road toward Red's, the Rev. Rice Roylott opened his window and got a whiff of a stench like a state park Port-o-Potty left alone too long. Like sulfur. Or Hell.

"Aaagh! Jeez!" he said out loud, rolling up the window and punching the heater fan knob as he slowed to a stop at Red's.

Red, breathless-- having tumbled down and across the field to meet the visitor-- recognized the car as he approached it. He felt less threatened and excited, less like his mother's great-grandfather, hunting along the flood-plain wilderness before the Kickapoo or the Illinois or Mackinaw rivers ever were named.

"Rev, what brings you out here? White White Witch getcha?" Red asked. "What's it been since you stopped by? A year ago? Trying to get me to come to church?"

"Yeah, well..."

"I didn't know who was comin', for a minute," Red said. "Thought I might become a fugitive. I've always thought of London, but I'd hate to leave the land."

"Jeez, how d'ya stand it?" Roylott said, waving his hand as he got out of his car.

"The smell? It's no worse than the site by church, is it? By Cassie's? B'sides, in spite of the lagoons-- or those slurry stores fulla crap at the finishers-- there are things worse than a stink."

"What could be worse than this?"

"Tryin' to get me started, Rev?" Red said. "Try imagining hundreds of Olympic-sized swimming pools with manure and urine 'mixed' with water. Try imagining being anywhere near when these fools and their sprayers shoot the manure mix 50 feet into the air, or inject it to the point it's toxic.

"Try to imagine damaged soil, no water, property values fallin' through the basement, that flesh-eatin' pfiesteria stuff."

"Ah, mmm," Roylott said. "Say, I hoped you'd be here. I... I hope I'm not bothering you, Red, but if you don't mind, I need an ear."

Red was silent.

"You heard about Rassendeal?"

"Rudy?"

"Ron."

"His kin?"

"His killing."

Their faces flushed. A moment passed. A mourning dove cooed.

"My wife died last night."

"God, Rice. I'm sorry."

"'preciate it. Actually, it wasn't unexpected, and it wasn't as terrible as we feared. We'd reached a... a reckoning, I guess. Forgave each other. For a lot of hurtful things. The visiting nurse from St. Francis was there, too. The wife, she went peaceful."

After several seconds of sighs, silent tears and lumps in throats, Red put his hand on Rice's shoulder.

"Forgiveness is tough," Red said. "I see 'Love your neighbor as yourself', but 'Love your enemy'? Jesus is tough."

"I know, I know. 'Turn the other cheek'? I've been slapped in the face, more than once. I've been kicked in the back side, over and over. I've turned the other cheek, but I'm flat out of cheeks."

"What can I do?" Red asked. "How do you feel?

"Relieved, freed. Guilty, ... gutted-- and a little awkward, to tell the truth. Maybe I don't need to talk. Maybe I need a change of scenery. Something."

The two men stood and stared blankly past each other.

Red said, "Bein' a 'heathen,' my mom had unorthodox prayers. One comforted me: 'The Great Spirit's in all things, in the air. The Great Spirit's our Father, the Earth our Mother. She nourishes us; she returns to us that which we put into the ground'."

"Potawatomie prayer?"

"Maybe. Maybe Mom prayer. Could be a Hallmark card."

"She doesn't sound like a heathen. She sounds God-fearing."

The minister walked over to a pile of twisted metal left over from a bin ripped from the edge of the meadow by a tornado that left the house and outbuildings untouched. He looked over the premises, his eyes locking on the restored red Farm-All F-20, an International Harvester tractor more than 50 years old.

"I don't mean this to be insulting, Red, but tell me," Roylott asked. "With all the modern technology-- computers and huge machines and genetically altered seeds and all that-- why do you seem so determined to hang on to what's... I dunno, old-fashioned?"

He surveyed the spread, seeing Red's green combine and pickup truck. In the shed were two old wooden wagons by a greased-up disc and a rusted, dented planter. They started walking to the house.

Shrugging, Red said, "That tractor was my grandpa's. It does the job. That truck is from 1950-- the year I was born; got it at an auction when a bank foreclosed on a farm.

"Chemical-resistant seeds, multi-ton harvesters with air conditioning and CD stereo, genetics, satellite data services-- it all can lure you from the dirt faster'n the meat monopolies promising producers easy money for doin' neighbors wrong," he continued. "Say, did you know the damned packinghouses have so much capacity, they could slaughter more than 400,000 hogs a day? And the daily kill's only about 360,000? Something's fishy.

"Or, not," he said. "Temptation tempers faith."

Roylott sniffed and nodded.

"Progress is fine, but nothin's planned anymore," Red said. "It's greed and speed. Everything's growing so fast-- I got a

Peoria phone number, an Edwards address, the neighbor kids ride the school bus to Elmwood and I shop in Hanna City and Farmington. I like being five minutes from the Interstate and taking it to town or over to Tazewell to Cassie's. But... what's bein' sacrificed?

"If we lose the land, the future could mean fish kills, wells poisoned," he added. "'sides, you get wrapped up in agri-BIZ, you end up like a bird in a building, trapped in a mall, going nowhere, feeding on crumbs: cinnamon buns, big cookies, caramel corn. Crap."

"Still, Red. Those overalls." He grinned. "Jeez."

Red straightened the straps on his Oshkosh denims and sighed.

"It's all still working the dirt," he said. "No amount of magic from Monsanto is gonna change that. As for these pants, they're comfy. Like the Hotel Pere Marquette, downtown."

"I don't getcha."

"Yeah," Red said. "Big ballroom."

●

"I still don't understand how you provoked Red," Cassie said.

"What's with your hand, anyway? Is he some sensitive sort, a troublemaker, like the guy who protested the Fighting Illini name?"

"No, not really. My partner thinks the Washington Redskins' name is barbarous, the Cleveland Indians stupid, and doesn't really care for the Illini-- or the Fighting Irish. But he's not offended by Braves or Chiefs. He says he figures those names are Native American versions of warriors or kings."

"All I know is, he lost it when I told him I'd traced our family to the Pawsitee tribe and mentioned my plan," Rudy said.

"I was just making small talk. Thought he'd find it interesting--preferable to the mega-farms you folks hate."

"Plan? First, Rudy, how'd you track your ancestry to Indians?"

"Family scrapbooks. Letters. It's a claim that's going to get me out of the used-car business and into the used-money trade."

"Oh?"

"Yassir. I'm going to open a land-based casino run by a Native American Indian: me," he said. "Right here in the tri-county. See, tribal governments can own and operate Indian gaming facilities, using the money for 'economic development.' Earnings are tax-free and operators aren't just protected by limited liability incorporation, they have what's called sovereign immunity."

"In other words, Indians can't be sued without their consent-- like government," Cassie said.

"Exactly. And all I know is, state government isn't unwilling to listen, and with its help, the National Indian Gaming Commission will OK it."

"But how--"

"My 'Equalizer'," Rudy said, stroking the gray duct tape around the cardboard box. "Soft-money campaign contributions."

"You're kidding," Cassie said. "Soft money, hard currency, wrong's wrong, Rudy. I know Mux is your pet legislator-- you even got him to hold out against all the other area lawmakers trying to hammer out a bill to control mega-farms. But apart from a law, what makes you think the economy can support a land-based casino?"

"Look, Cass, gambling boats are failing all along the Mississippi. Besides, gaming and Peoria just go together.

"There was a time-- we were kids then-- when this was a

wide-open area," he continued, nostalgia in his voice. "Lottery, off-track betting and riverboats all stole the decent vices."

"Decent?" Cassie asked. "What about the indecent vices? What's that? Prostitution? Protection? Drugs? "

Rudy chuckled.

Cassie figured Red didn't like the casino scheme, but she wasn't sure about Ron.

"How'd your brother feel about this Indian nonsense?"

"It's not nonsense," Rudy said. "All I know is, Ron's gone. He's always been there for me. I may have been the brains in the family, but he was the guts. We had differences, sure, what brothers don't? It always worked out somehow.

"He was old-fashioned. Taught Bible class, f'r crissakes. So he objected to the 'sin' of gambling," Rudy continued. "'Course, he had no reservations, so to speak, about polluting. That's all God's plan for man's dominion over the Earth and animals, he'd say."

"Aren't Indian lands protected?"

"Sure, right. All I know is, if there are Indian mounds around, fine, we'll work around them. There are acres of strip-mine ground available next to PNI-- here and in Peoria County.

"Right next to the stink? Isn't that stupid?"

"It'll be a casino, Cassie, not a campground," he said. "No one stands outside a casino. The action's inside."

"Well, I've had too much action here. You're going outside."

"But my car's clear down by the church."

"Take my car; key's in it. Leave it at the church."

While Cassie walked Rudy to the door, she noticed her phone machine-- catching calls all night-- blinked like the timer on some weapon of mass destruction. She opened the front door.

"Rudy, this is a scam. And even if you're 1/64th Pawsitee, just because you have the right to do something doesn't mean it's the right thing to do. And the cash for Mux-- what? Mux' bucks..."

"Lawmakers live on money, Cassie. The capitol building glitters with a silver roof, not white for purity."

She shut the door and punched the phone machine.

Ostrogoth, her lawyer, called back. Sheafhecker left a message. Newspaper and TV reporters left numbers. And Rice Roylott called, concerned about her, he said. And, his wife died.

●

Seated at his kitchen table, Red poured decaf coffee for Rice.

"Thanks. You exhausted from the harvest, Red?"

"I've never needed much sleep. Helps when you got a job off the farm."

Rice nodded and said, "Feel it? Storm could be a gully washer. Feel it? Like tension."

"It might be," Red said. "Time was, folks lived in harmony with the land and each other. Corn farmer, hog man, it didn't matter. Respect. The country's best farmers and best corn-growing soil helped make hogs 'mortgage makers.' No more."

"How'd you end up here, Red?"

"I bought this place, 80 acres, when I worked at Cat. After we went on strike in the '80s-- before the demon Downsizing became a meaningless media term-- I got laid off, called back, laid off, forgotten. Cassie's dad helped me, hired me to give 'em a hand."

Lightning flashed. Red and Rice were quiet for several seconds, then Red said, "My Mom taught me to praise God and pray for protection and strength, wisdom and health. She said people shouldn't ask God for vengeance, that He doesn't care about our petty quarrels. But sometimes we could seek vengeance ourselves."

"Red, what you said about temptation tempering faith?"

"Yeah?"

"I gave in," Rice said, "I failed my faith."

"Me, too."

Shaking his head, Rice looked up, adding, "Brother, I'm in trouble."

"Pastor, we all are."

Thunder boomed like a cannon, and the rain seemed to fall in sheets.

3
MAD MUX

David Everson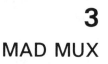

"In the County of Cook," Ross Miller said, "the dead elect the living. But in Tazewell County, the *living* elect the *dead.*"

Although she was used to his word games, Maggie Lynch knew her (tor)mentor expected her to appear puzzled. And this time, she was. "Yo, Miller," she said. "Explain."

He peered quizzically over half-shell glasses. "State Senator Mortimer Mux's been brain dead for years. He is also given to insane rants-- totally losing it-- on the Senate floor. Some wags call him 'Mad Mux.' Trust me, when he slimed into the Illinois General Assembly, the average I.Q. dropped from 'mentally challenged' to 'sub-moron'."

"I don't think 'slime' is a verb," she said, tossing her auburn hair back away from her emerald eyes.

"In Illinois, maybe it should be."

She figured this was going somewhere, but was clueless as to the ultimate destination.

"Like-- Miller-- what's your point?"

She was standing with her back against the door of the tiny *Herald-Star* press office on the mezzanine of the state capitol building. He was resting in an easy chair, looking like the cat that swallowed the canary. He pointed a trigger finger at her. "Lynch, I'm sending you to cover his press conference today as preparation to do a little 'Muxraking'." He grinned as he made little quotation marks with his fingers around his pun.

"What's the subject of this press conference?"

"With Mux, there's only ever one subject: himself." He grinned. "Oh, you mean the substance. I'll get to that in a minute. First, some background. Mux is in a tight re-election race." Miller shook his gray head sorrowfully. "Guy's a throwback to the bad old days of the General Assembly. Holds the world's record in the neck flush. Lots of fistfights on the floor of the Senate. Never saw a trough he couldn't get his snout into. Plus, he's the biggest defender of that racist Indian mascot over at the U of I. Worst of all, in recent years, he's been the best friend of those mega-hog farms. That's why he's in political hot water in the district. His opponent is making a stink-- no pun-- out of that. I want to help take him down." He paused, working his eyebrows like Groucho Marx. "One other thing: Mux's also a Lincoln impersonator. Performs all over downstate."

"Abe must be turning over."

Miller nodded. "Big time."

Miller was the veteran Capital correspondent of the Chicago *Herald-Star*. In a real sense, he was a foreign correspondent because Chicago regarded downstate a whole other country. And vice-versa. Lynch-- from Chicago-- was his intern and he didn't want her to forget it. He threw her a change up.

"Did you hear about the severed-head-in-the-pumpkin incident in Tazewell County?"

"Of course. It even made NPR. But what does that have to do with Mux?"

His response was another *non sequitur.* "Lynch, Native Americans can operate gambling casinos on their own lands. With sovereign immunity. Free from government regulations and taxes."

"Cool," she said. But her expression said: so what?

He looked at her over his half-glasses, a trace of a smile on his lips. "But what does that have to do with policing Mortimer Mux?"

She nodded. "Yeah."

"He wants to create a Little Las Vegas-- Native American style-- in Tazewell County. That's what this press conference is about."

She sighed. "Daley, the Lesser, couldn't get that done in my kind of town. What makes Mux think he has more clout than Daley?"

"One of his land-owning constituents claims to be a Native-American."

She drew a question mark in the air. "So?"

"That head in the pumpkin? It belonged to the brother of this guy who claims to be an Indian."

She looked totally baffled now. She shook her hair out of her eyes again. "Like-- what's the connection?"

"That's what I want *you* to find out. And then there's the matter of the 'White White Witch'."

Her jaw dropped. "Huh?"

"A naked woman riding around central Illniois on a Harley-Davidson. On holidays. April Fool's. Lincoln's birthday. Fourth of July."

"What"s she got to do with this?"

"Damned if I know, but it's an interesting coincidence that Halloween is coming up. You might luck into a sighting if the

Mux story takes you to Tazewell County. Anyhow, Mux is putting in a bill to allow this 'Indian' to open a land-based casino." He indicated his skepticism by making quotation marks again with his fingers.

She said, "Hello, Miller! That's nuts. We already have too many riverboat casinos downstate. Isn't there already one in East Peoria?"

He nodded. "Mortimer may be dumb but that doesn't mean he hasn't learned how to put in a 'fetcher bill'."

"Excuse me?"

He looked at her over his glasses again. "Lynch, I'm not sure you're well enough versed in Illinois legislative politics to cover this story."

"How complicated can it be?" With a perverse sense of pride, she said, "I've covered Council Wars."

"Child," he said in a tone she had grown to hate, "Chicago and downstate are in different galaxies. Anyway, a 'fetcher bill' isn't *supposed* to pass. It's supposed to 'fetch' a legal bribe-- a.k.a. a *campaign contribution*-- to the sponsor to kill it. Mux probably figures the riverboat casino interests will contribute to his flagging campaign if he lets the bill die a decent death by sending it to 'interim study,' the graveyard of bills nobody really wants to see pass."

"Isn't 'legal bribe' a contradiction in terms?"

Miller sighed. "Not in Illinois. Here it's almost impossible to have a campaign finance scandal because anything and everything's legal. Anyone can give any amount of money to any politician for any purpose as long as there is not an explicit quid pro quo. Even Mux knows that."

●

So that's how Maggie Lynch-- intern in the Civic Affairs Reporting Program of Lincoln Heritage University in Springfield-- found herself covering Mortimer Mux's first and last press conference at the state capitol.

Mux stood self-importantly in front of a podium, speaking in an oily voice.

"The state of Illinois is sending more bucks into Tazewell County than it's taking out in taxes. You can't get blood from a turnip."

To Lynch, Mux didn't look any dopier than the average Chicago alderman she had covered before deciding to get her Master's at LHU. He was tall, in his mid-sixties, with a full head of iron-gray hair swept into a kind of pompadour. He wore a dark suit, a white shirt and a gray striped tie. He spoke from notes, his voice surprisingly reedy, unpleasant to the ear. Now he smiled coldly.

"I've been pretty good at bringing home the bacon for the county. My support for mega-hog farms is well-known." He paused, sensing his own words opened a subject he'd rather not have to defend. Suddenly, he looked like Nixon just before the resignation, pale gray eyes shifting uncontrollably.

"I know they have their critics, but we are well on the way to the technology to get rid of the stin-- ah, the odor." He quickly switched to safer ground. "I've brought in more roads, more bridges and more projects for the district than anyone ever did. What I'm asking for is something quite different. Not a hand-out, a hand up. Something productive. I want the state to let us determine our own fate by backing my proposal for a land-based casino in Tazewell County."

Lynch sat in the back row of the small blue room provided for press conferences in the state capitol. *Productive?* she thought, but she was a little timid about asking questions with all the old pros around. The room was located on the mezzanine next to the offices of the various news services. There were about a dozen reporters covering Mux's announcement of his plan. She saw several of her colleagues snickering as he spoke. If Mux noticed, he did not let on.

"One of my constituents is a red-- ah, Indian, who owns land in the county. He is asking for his right to open a casino and I am supporting him with legislation to that effect. If we get a land-based casino, it will not only help Indians, it will lead to the resurgence of Tazewell County. If we build a little Las Vegas, they will come. Who is *they*?"

Are, Lynch said to herself.

Mux answered his own question. "Tourists and investors. We will need motels, hotels, restaurants, shopping malls. The revenue base of the county will multiply. We will need better roads and bridges for people to get to the casino. That will create jobs, lots of jobs. And jobs mean a larger tax base. More sales tax for the state. More income tax for the state. More income for the good citizens of the tri-county region. I don't see how anyone can oppose this proposal. To be honest, this is a win-win for the state and for the people of Tazewell County."

A reporter from Peoria didn't wait for Mux to finish. He cut in. "What tribe is involved in this scheme?" The way he said, "scheme," he might as well have said: this *scam*.

Mux was not flustered. "The Pawsitees."

The reporter said, "I thought they were extinct."

Mux shook his head with confidence. "It turns out that is not so."

"How many survive?"

Now Mux looked uncomfortable. He turned to an

obviously nervous staff member at his side who shrugged. Mux said, "I don't have that information."

The reporter said, "I'm told there is only one, the last of the Pawsitees, Rudy Rassendeal, brother of the late Ron Rassendeal of mega-hog farm fame. And I also hear that Rudy's claim to Native American blood is highly dubious."

Mux looked irritated. "No comment," he snapped.

Another reporter asked, "Isn't it true that Rassendeal is one of your biggest campaign contributors""

Mux held up his right hand as if taking an oath. "Frankly, I make it a point not to know whom my contributors are."

There was stunned silence. *Who*, Lynch said to herself. The Illinois General Assembly, home of the whopper, she thought. Then a third reporter asked, "What's to keep other Illinois tribes from asking for the same deal?"

Mux smiled, spreading his hands. "Nothing. I wish them well."

Lynch tentatively raised her hand, but Mux paid no attention. The reporter from Peoria said, "Your re-election?"

Mux looked wary. "What about it?"

"Our most recent poll has you behind by five percentage points."

Two spots of red flared on Mux's cheeks. "The only poll that counts is on election day."

The reporter continued, "My point is that this might seem to some like a desperate attempt-- a publicity stunt-- to revive a dying candidacy."

Mux's whole face flamed. He balled his fists. His staff member put a restraining hand on Mux. He wrenched away, taking a step toward the reporter. Then, with an obvious act of will, he controlled himself. "No more questions," he declared.

He stalked from the room.

Mad Mux.

Lynch caught up with him at the rail on the third floor next to the House chambers. This was where the lobsters-- the name for lobbyists in Illinois-- practiced the persuasive arts on legislators. "Representative Mux""

He turned, anger still on his face. "*What*?"

"I'd like a one-on-one interview."

He glared at her. "I said, 'no more questions.' What part of 'no' don't you understand?" Then he paused, ran his gaze up and down her body, pale gray eyes undressing her. She visibly shuddered. "I've always been a sucker for red hair and green eyes. On second thought, let's make a deal," he said, licking his fleshy lips. "Tell you what, little lady. I'm busy this afternoon. I'll talk to you if you will accompany me to the annual Lincoln Halloween Ball tonight as my date. It would be a good history lesson for you. What do you say?" He winked at her.

To Lynch's eye, he was practically drooling. Let's not go there, she thought. But then her journalistic instincts took hold. "Cool," she said.

●

Mux made a pretty traditional Lincoln in long black coat and stove pipe hat. He leaned into Lynch's space-- smelling like a hog farm, she thought-- and whispered that she looked "fetching." He had her pinned against the statue of a woman on the ground floor of the capitol. Lynch slid a good two feet away from him. They stood in the rotunda, the location of the Halloween Party. A small jazz band-- with all the members dressed as Lincoln-- played Dixieland so loudly that it was hard to hear any conversation unless you were at closer quarters than she ever wanted to be with Mux.

Four corridors met at the rotunda. Way above her, she could see the stained glass of the interior of the capitol dome. On the second and third floors, there were busts of famous Illinois politicians looking down on the spectacle below. She thought it was like being caught in "Honest Abe's Madhouse of Distorting Mirrors." Swirling all around her were fat Lincolns, skinny Lincolns, short Lincolns, tall Lincolns, Lincolns with spiked hair, Lincolns with earrings, Lincolns with tattoos and Lincolns in drag. All were sipping from wineglasses, sampling party snacks and conversing (she imagined) about Lincoln's lost love, Ann Rutledge, his mad wife, Mary Todd, and the veracity of Herndon's life of Lincoln.

She was the only one in the room not dressed as Lincoln, although she could have sworn she had caught a glimpse of someone in Native American garb down at the end of the long north corridor. Black Hawk?

She wore a blue blazer, white blouse, red skirt, white hose and blue high-heeled shoes. I *do* look fetching, she thought. Which is probably a big mistake. *What won't I do for this interview?*

Mux moved closer to her and said, "Do you know the story of how Lincoln stole the state capitol from Vandalia?"

Duh, she thought. "No," she lied, batting her eyes. "Tell me." He did, at considerable length, although she could only catch about half of it due to the band. When he paused to catch his breath, she asked, "Aren't mega-hog farms environmentally dangerous?"

He moved closer to her. "Let's not talk shop, little lady."

"What about the run-off pollution getting into wells, rivers and lakes?"

He ignored that and tried to put his arm around her. She edged away.

"Some people in the pressroom," she said, "were saying that your casino deal is a 'fetcher bill'."

The twin red spots on his cheeks made an encore appearance. "Frankly, my dear, they are full of crap... If you insist on conducting business, we are going to have to go to my office on the third floor." He winked as he had that afternoon and tried to pat her backside. She dodged. He said, "All they have here is wine. I have a bottle of something with a little more kick."

"Cool," she said. Thank God I brought my pepper spray, she thought.

●

Mux had her backed up against the desk of his office, trying to kiss her, mumbling his unswerving devotion to her. She was fumbling on the desk with one hand for a weapon while fending him off with the other. The assault had knocked her purse-- with the pepper spray-- to the floor. Her hand closed around something rectangular with a surprising heft. She swung it against Mux's left ear. He bellowed and released her, moaning.

Still gripping the object of her deliverance, she fled the office and reached the rail, pausing for breath. Mux lurched out of the office, shambling in her direction, cursing. Suddenly furious, she stood her ground, brandishing her weapon. He saw what she held and lunged for it. Just then, he grunted and toppled to the floor on his face. He's drunker than I thought, she said to herself.

Then she saw there was a feathered arrow in the middle of his back. It must have been launched from above, she thought.

She glanced at the fourth floor. Again she thought she caught a glimpse of a figure in Indian garb that disappeared into the gloom much like a vanishing mirage.

She looked once more at Mux. The arrow had a note attached.

Lynch faced a dilemma of journalistic ethics: scream for help-- Mux might not be dead and maybe it was not too late to catch the archer-- or check the note first, call Miller to tell him she had an exclusive interview with a murder victim, and then scream?

She knelt. The note said: "Revenge."

As she stood to head for the phone to talk to Miller, she noticed her "weapon" still in her hand. It was a shoe box wrapped with gray duct tape. She ripped off the tape, opened it and took in the contents.

"Way cool," she said.

4
LAGOON
INTERLUDE

Jerry Klein

Cassie had slept most of the day away. Now-- leaning on the sill of an open window and breathing in the cool night air-- her mind reeled with a flood of unanswered questions. The wind was from the northwest, the sky had cleared, and there wasn't a trace of that gagging, sulfurous odor from the hellish lagoons of Porklips Now, Inc.

Lagoons, she thought idly. The word at one time would have conjured imaged of some South Seas island with azure waters, young bronzed men paddling their thin, dugout canoes, women in sarongs, and the rich, heady scents of Bougainvillea and Frangipani.

But not now. Now the lagoon meant a horrendous caldron of pig manure so potent that it could peel paint. And when the wind was right (or wrong), the stench spread across the land like evil, consuming tentacles.

Not tonight. Not yet. There were the late October smells of apples and grapes, dry, rustling corn fields and... pumpkins.

Pumpkins, she thought. What crazed genius had managed to behead that sad and miserable excuse for a man, Ron Rassendeal, to whom she was lately betrothed? Ugh. And then apparently encase his head inside of a pumpkin, of all things, and hurl it through the night right through her window-- with the aid of some powerful device, maybe the Aludium Q36 Pumpkin Modulator, which she had seen impressively displayed last month at the Morton Pumpkin Festival.

It had been phenomenal. Hundreds of people had flocked to a bare field to watch the pumpkin-throwing contest, and for many of them it had been like watching artillery. The orange projectiles simply moved too fast for the eye to follow. There had been devices like Roman ballista, which flung pumpkins some distance. There had been other contraptions to "chuck" pumpkins: huge slingshots, odd-shaped catapults and this 100-foot-long modulator, which looked like an oil derrick on a flatbed truck. The modulator had a great, whooshing buildup, followed by a grand release that-- depending on where an onlooker stood-- sounded like a rocket igniting at the Kennedy Space Center, or a sneeze. Off the pumpkin would go.

But with a head inside, who could calculate the path of the projectile so accurately as to hit the bull's eye of her window? Obviously, this was no dumbbell. She concluded that this probably ruled out Rudy Rassendeal, who was not only unlikely to behead his brother, but lacked the intelligence and the planning skills to bring off so bizarre a scheme. If, indeed, the modulator had been used, somebody would have to steal it, tow it within a mile or so, and shoot the pumpkin/head toward her house. Incredible.

And this seemed to leave an almost equally unlikely gaggle of suspects, Cassie mused. The Rev. Rice Roylott? Where was the motive here? Certainly not jealousy.

Revenge? Now, here was a key word. But what did it mean? What could that crazed naked motorcyclist racing through the night have to do with the pumpkin modulator, Porklips Now's lagoons, or the grisly, severed head of Ron Rassendeal? The White White Witch sounded so harmless, so... well, nutty. Lady Godiva on a Harley.

Then there was State Sen. Mortimer Mux, whose dealings with Porklips and the Rassendeals might have been dark and sinister enough to cause the hatching of some ingenious plan. He wouldn't have pulled the trigger, as such, maybe, but he had the power to manipulate people. Yes, he could have arranged for the modulator to be stolen, the head to be severed, and even Rudy to be flung head-long-- as it were-- into the lagoon.

Except Mux was apparently dead. At least that was the report on the 10 p.m. news-- sketchy though it was. A well-coiffed anchor read a brief bulletin that Mux was found outside his Capitol office with an arrow in his back, discovered by some reporter named Lynch. After alerting viewers with such a sensational teaser and promising details later, the anchor added nothing. They cut to commercials, the weather, chit chat, sports, more chit chat and a closing reminder that the TV station would follow the breaking Mux story and share it tomorrow.

Maybe the morning paper would have details-- if they could find room among all their features about good deeds, AIDS marches, and people with button collections. Surely they would think a bizarre murder of a senator by bow and arrow ought to merit something more than a few paragraphs on an inside page.

Bow and arrow. Indian. Casino. By now, Cassie's mind was spinning like a gambling boat's slot machine trying to click three bars into place.

What she needed was some common link.

The casino and the Indian. The Indian and the lagoons, full of pig waste. Revenge. That word covered a lot of territory. It also was the message left by the White White Witch from her dark and speeding Harley. It could have been a message left by an Indian over the fact that the treasured land had been despoiled, or the casino stalled. The only Native American she knew personally was Red, her partner, her helper, her friend.

No, she thought, I know Rudy, who at least claimed to be a Pawsitee Indian. And he wouldn't crusade against his family's own interest in the mega-hog farm, much less go about dressed like a brave and loosing an arrow that found its target in the back of his own Senator Mux. That simply didn't figure.

Which Indian? Unknown or real or phony? There probably hadn't been a real Indian in Tazewell County since the time of Black Hawk. And who was Lynch? Was the reporter a suspect or a witness? After all, what could bring a journalist to Mux mere moments before some mysterious arrow found its way into the sebaceous fat of the senator's porcine back?

Pigs again.

Suddenly, Cassie winced. The wind had changed. It had veered around and was coming out of the Southwest. No longer were there the late evening scents of fall in central Ilinois: burning leaves from some distant bonfire, the winey mingling of apples and wild grapes and the scent of the rich, black earth. Now it was pig manure, and its stink crept across the land like a plague, first flowing into the low-lying areas like a septic fog, then-- stirred sluggishly by the wind-- permeating everything.

A plague. Cassie wondered if Job had experienced anything quite like this. Her Bible made no mention of the nauseating, eye-burning odor of pigs afflicting Job, or, for that matter, the Pharoahs of Egypt who-- because they had kept the chosen people captive for so long-- experienced their own punishment. She felt like one of the chosen people now, wandering in her own lifeless desert, with no end in sight. No manna. No answers. Only confusion and ignorance, liberation mixed with betrayal.

The house and farm had been for sale, then willed to her if she remained, effectively locking her in a fight with PNI. And with PNI's purgatorial smell, like ammonia and the effluvium of some giant septic tank. No, worse. Arising throughout central Illinois, Porklips Now and its stink-- its stain-- was always there, lurking behind the next change of the wind, threatening to make the region an Arthurian Wasteland.

It was like going to hell one sense at a time, she thought, the recoiling nose first, the stinging eyes next...

She shut the window, turning the metal hasp on the sash, lockng it tight. It was dark in her living room, except for the red eye of her answering machine blinking devilishly. Cassie yawned as she walked to the machine and touched the message button. There were several calls-- Red checking in, Sheafhecker, Ostrogoth, Sgt. Lynn letting her know that the Modulator was, indeed, missing.

Then Cassie froze.

The voice was unmistakeable, grating and unctuous. It was Mux, who was supposed to be either seriously wounded or dead.

"Miss Canine," he said, mispronouncing it K-9. "This is Senator Mortimer Mux here... and I understand you're in a heap of trouble over the... mysterious murder of Ron Rassendeal. I may be able to help you. I won't be at a number you can reach me for a while-- right now I must put on my Lincoln costume for a Halloween party in the Capitol-- but why don't you give me a call in the morning and maybe we can come up with... some answers.

"Bye-bye."

5

THE BRIDGES
OF McLEAN COUNTY

Julie Kistler

As Halloween edged closer, bittersweet autumn dreams swept through Central Illinois.

High on a hill near a park, the woman known as the White, White Witch snuggled her pale, porcelain curves deeper into the white, white bedlinens in the white, white bedroom of her white, white house. As her dream took her spinning through Greater Peoria on her motorcycle, she felt the letters emblazoned on her ample bottom-- "Heav'n has no rage, like love to hatred turn'd. Nor hell a fury, like a woman scorn'd. Congreve."-- tingle and burn, as hot as the fireworks over the Civic Center during March Madness.

Near Mackinaw, Sam Sheafhecker pressed his cheek into his pillow, hand-embroidered with little lassoes and horsies by his Grammy Sheafhecker. He was dreaming a fantastic dream, all about a mysterious woman in white who beckoned to him, not five feet away, with a glimmer of motorcycle headlights casting a romantic glow on the back of her head...

In rural Peoria County, in his hard, narrow bed, Red Pavlow stirred in his sleep, moving his feet to the beat of distant drums, as his tribal ancestors called for war against the despoilers of their land.

Over in Tazewell County, Cassie Canine was once more asleep. She giggled in the midst of a luscious dream, dog-paddling through a huge vat of cooked, warm pumpkin pie filling, somewhere at the processing plant in Morton. Thick, sweet, fragrant with nutmeg and cinnamon, it was just how she envisioned Heaven.

Even in a fantasy, she didn't dare eat any of it, of course -- those calories were like sin on a biscuit. Maybe if she just took a tiny nibble...

"Cassie?" She woke up angrily, not ready to leave her lovely dream behind. "Cassie? Wake up!"

The Rev. Rice Roylott was standing in her bedroom with an open window blowing a chill behind him. It was the same window the head of Ron Rassendeal had come shooting through only a few days ago, wrapped in a pumpkin shell like one of the Wise Men toting frankincense to Jesus. She'd just had it fixed, and now the Reverend was playing second-story man, climbing in her windows to press his unwelcome suit.

Cassie leapt up from the bed, keeping a quilt tucked securely around her Greyhound-thin frame. "So you've stooped to breaking into my house now? And what is that you're carrying?"

But she already knew. Her food-starved brain could recognize the tantalizing aroma of warm pumpkin pie faster than David's slingshot slew Goliath. She staggered backwards, reeling from temptation.

"I made it for you," he said with a lopsided smile. "From scratch."

Cassie tried to remain strong. "You know I don't eat that kind of thing," she murmured, licking her lips. "Do you know how many fat grams there are in crust?"

"Uh, no." But there was a hopeful light on his handsome face. "It's my gift to you, my dear Cassie. I don't have a whole lot of worldly goods, so I have to use what I have around."

"And what you have around is pumpkin pie filling?" she asked suspiciously. "What was it, an old dented can that fell off a truck coming from Morton?"

"Nope. No can. I said I made it from scratch, didn't I?"

From scratch. From a pumpkin. Once again, her mind fed her an image of Ron Rassendeal's head in its pumpkin shell. Somebody carved the guts out of that pumpkin. And somebody had to dispose of those guts.

Suddenly resolute, she reached out and grabbed the pie, veering around Roylott and making a beeline for the stairs. "Thanks," she called over her shoulder. "I'm putting it on ice. Until..."

Until she could get somebody to test the contents of that pie against the shards still left in her hallway. Until she knew for sure whether the Reverend was cooking up evidence in that cozy kitchen of his.

"But Cassie-- wait," he said, following her down the stairs. "I brought your car back from the church. Wait! Cassie?"

At the bottom of the stairs, Cassie propped open the front door, leaving him no choice but to depart. He did, silently.

Rid of Roylott, Cassie set the pie in the freezer just as the phone rang. She let it ring, but when her machine picked up, she could hear the long, shrill beep of a fax. She raced into her office to catch the sheets as they spit out. "What now?" she asked out loud. After last night's cryptic message from that crooked arrow, Mortimer Mux, she was full up on missives from the Great Beyond.

It wasn't good news.

"Hellfire," she muttered, already dialing her partner, Red Pavlow. She didn't waste time on preliminaries. "Get over here on the double. Mortimer Mux was shot with an arrow last night in Springfield. He's still hanging on by a thread, but it doesn't look good. A cub reporter, Maggie somebody, was there when he went down, and she just faxed me with some of the details, thought maybe I could help fill in a few blanks. It seems old Muxie boy was carrying a shoebox full of cash when he got hit. The shoebox was for a Big Ol' Boy Workboot, size 13EEE, which I happen to know is Rudy Rassendeal's size. And about that arrow..." She paused.

"Go on," he said grimly.

"It looks just like the ones hangin' over your fireplace, Red. Pawsitee, right? And the only man I know with Pawsitee arrows is you."

When the doorbell rang 10 minutes later, she thought Red must've broken land-speed records or something. But instead, she saw the eager face of Sam Sheafhecker, errand boy and P.I. wannabe, still wearing his pajama tops under his overalls, clutching a Polaroid in one hand.

"Miss Canine, I'm real sorry to be waking you up and all, but I got me a clue!" he said proudly, waving the photo.

"At the moment, Sam, we are up to our hips in 'em, deeper than ol' Rudy when he fell into the cesspool at the mega-hog farm." Frowning, she let him in. "What's this all about?"

"The Aludium Q36 Pumpkin Modulator. The chukker! It's been spotted, Miss C. Over to McLean County!"

Quickly, Cassie grabbed the photo. Although it showed two older ladies in flowered dresses smirking for the camera, in the

background you could make out a small bridge, and next to it...
the long arm of the famous pumpkin punter.

"Where'd you get this?" she demanded.

He launched into a windy, folksy explanation, something
about old ladies going to Bloomington for a tour of a candy
factory and ending up "loster than a polecat at the Santy Claus
parade." They saw some goofy little covered bridge, stopped to
take their picture with it, and spotted the Aludium in the
background, after which they rushed right over to tell Sam.

When he paused for breath, Cassie jumped in. "You're
gonna have to retrace their steps, Sam. We need to find that
Modulator."

"But, Miss Canine..." Sam's face grew pink. "That's over
in McLean County. I ain't never been out of Tazewell. I heard
tell they've got that Veterans Parkway over there, not fit for man
nor beast."

"Get a grip, Sheafheacker. We got more clues coming in
than Abraham begat tribes. You've got to help out."

"But, Miss Canine..." He screwed up his face. "My ma
took her truck over to Canton, and all I got to drive is the
combine."

"Good enough. I'm going to need my car." She gave him
her best motivational stare. "Fire up the combine, take one of
my cameras and a notebook, and get goin', big boy."

Sam hesitated, long enough for Red to come busting through
the back door. "Show me," he said tersely, his jaw tight with
anger. All it took was one quick look at the faxed page. "It's
genuine, all right. Someone is trying to make it look like an
Indian did this." He straightened. "Someone is trying to frame
one of my people."

"Red, I hate to tell you, but you're the only one of your

people left around here. 'Cept Rudy, of course, but we all know that's a big lie." Cassie patted his flannel-shirted arm, absently noting once more how strong and muscled he was. Red traveled a lonely path, and she'd never understood why. The woman who snared him would be lucky indeed. "Red, that arrow points right to you."

"If you think, for one minute, that I did this, defiling a perfectly good arrow in the swinish flesh of Mortimer Mux--"

"'Course not, Red. But that's why I'm going to have to get down there and see what they've got. You can't go-- they'll figure out in a New York minute that you're the only guy around here with Pawsitee arrows at his beck and call." She frowned. "I'll go. And Sam's hot on the trail of the Modulator. So that leaves you to take the Reverend's pumpkin pie over to the agriculture lab in Peoria to do DNA testing."

"DNA testing?" he asked doubtfully. "On a pumpkin pie?"

"I've got a hunch that pie matches my pumpkin shards. And if it does..."

Red finished softly, "Then Reverend Roylott has a lot to answer for."

Red grabbed the pie and foraged out in the hallway until he found a piece of dessicated pumpkin shell. Without a word, he hopped in his truck and made for the highway. Pushing a protesting Sheafheacker ahead of her, Cassie took off on her own, bound and determined to find that arrow and figure out who was trying to frame her partner.

"But Miss C," Sam tried one last time. "I ain't never been out of Tazewell County..."

•

Sam Sheafhecker was good and tired of people in their

dad-blamed cars honking at him. He and his combine were going as fast as they could.

He still hadn't spotted anything like the Modulator or the covered bridge in the picture, and he was getting hungry. When he saw the name "Rassendeal" on a mailbox, he pulled into the long gravel driveway quick. "Rhiney & Bonita Rassendeal," the mailbox said. He'd heard of Ron, now known throughout the area as the Great Pumpkin Head, and his brother Rudy, a rascal if ever there was one. But no "Rhiney." Still, there weren't too many Rassendeals around, so he doubted this was a coincidence.

The mailbox had a fat plastic pig affixed to the top, with "the Senator" written across its flank.

"Excuse me, ma'am," he said politely, doffing his feed cap at the woman in the faded dress who came to the door. "Can you tell me if you've seen a--"

"Say no more," she interrupted, grabbing his arm and hauling him into her kitchen. "I know who you are and why you're here, my weary traveler, my mystical stranger, my lone wolf, my restless drifter. You are a man who knows no bounds, a panther uncaged, a man whose soul is so deep it reflects the light of a thousand suns."

"Excuse me, ma'am," he said uneasily, "but I think you've mistaken me for someone else. I'm just looking for a little red bridge, one of them covered kind--"

"I knew it!" she cried. "When you said 'bridge' something leapt inside me, something primal and raw, something that speaks to me like the rain and makes me listen, something that makes me wonder if I should've thrown the tuna salad away a day earlier, something that says..." She moistened her lips and spoke in a breathy tone. "Something that says this is a man who can take your life on a tilt-a-whirl and hold you upside-down until you puke."

"That ain't me--"

"Of course it is." She gazed at her kitchen table, running a loving hand over the deep dip worn in the middle of it. "I've had a lot of mysterious strangers pass this way. I know one when I see one."

Sam's eyes widened. "And you fed the mysterious strangers on your table there?" he asked hopefully.

She laughed, a gay tinkle like bells. "No, mio caro. I made love to them on this table!"

"Made...?" He choked. "On a table? Why, that's unhealthy. And I thought you was married. To a Rassendeal."

She shrugged. "So? All he cares for is toting his mega-hog, the Senator, to festivals to show him off."

"Mega-hog? Is this a mega-hog farm?" Funny, he couldn't smell a thing.

"Yes, I suppose." Bonita waved a careless hand. "But we have just the one. Mega-hog, I mean. The Senator."

"Why's he named that?"

Her eyes grew misty once more. "My husband, Rhiney, he fell out with his brothers years ago. Bad blood. They got everything and we got nothing. All we had was the small pig. We kept him here, in the kitchen, in a box. And one day, I had the TV on, and some Senator from Champaign was there, squealing and carrying on about losing the high school basketball tournament to Peoria. It was as if the pig recognized a kindred spirit. He stood right up in his box, squealing just like the Senator. So that's what we named him."

She smiled again, still fingering that table. "He's quite the mega-hog now. Won all kinds of ribbons, and taken my husband away, leaving me free to find my destiny with mysterious strangers. You know," she said fondly, "there are a lot of festivals around these parts. Why, there's the Pumpkin Festival, the Sweetcorn, the Broomcorn, the Creamed Corn, the Candy Corn, the Apple and Pork, the Pork and Apple, the Pork, the Apple--"

Sam was getting mighty hungry. "So, listen, ma'am, you ever seen a covered bridge around here?"

"I know the bridge, caro mio." She snuggled up close, winding herself around his bicep, grinning up at him.

"My name ain't Carl, ma'am. It's Sam."

"No, you silly boy. I said, 'caro mio.' My beloved. It's Italian."

He peered down at her. "Are you Eye-talian?"

"Once, when I was young, I worked as a waitress at an Italian restaurant in Toluca." She gazed into space. "Ah, those were my salad days."

Sam was beginning to think Bonita Rassendeal was a few chickens short of a coop. "So what about this here bridge?"

"Down the road," she murmured. "At Rudy's little hobby farm. He builds toys like that bridge."

"Rudy? Rudy Rassendeal? He's got a place over here, too?"

"Oh, why do you distract me so?" She gazed into his eyes. "I wish to talk of destiny and Lady of Spain on the accordion and long, slow, sweet kisses under a dusty, red-orange-pink sunset--"

"I'm sorry, ma'am, but I ain't got time."

"All right. If you must." She cocked a thumb over her shoulder. "Down the road. Two miles. But you come back sometime, y'hear? Me and my kitchen table... will be waiting."

But Sam's mind was swimming with clues. Another

57

Rassendeal, one who'd fallen out with his brothers. Rudy, hiding a secret farm in McLean County. He screeched his combine to a stop.

"God almighty," he whispered. There was no Aludium Q36 to be seen. But there was a tiny covered bridge, just like in the picture. And there were deep grooves in the mud next to it, grooves that would fit a Modulator like fork tines on a peanut butter cookie.

Sam stooped to take in as much as he could. A pumpkin shard. He wrapped it in his handkerchief and stuck it carefully in his pocket. And a shoe print.

Sam whistled. "Why, that there's from a Big Ol' Boy workboot," he said. "Size 13EEE. From Farm & Fleet."

If there was one thing he knew, it was the wares at Farm & Fleet. He took a quick Polaroid of the footprint and jumped back into his cab.

He needed to get back to the safety of Tazewell County on the double. He had plenty of tales to tell.

6
FRIENDS
IN LOW PLACES

Nancy Atherton

Cassie Canine stood at the living room window and stared out across 300 acres of bean stubble. She'd been born and raised a flatlander. She loved the broad horizon, the wide sweep of ever-changing sky. Here she could watch the storms roll in-- and identify a passing pickup before it came within five miles of her farmhouse. Cassie liked to see what was coming. She had no hankering for roiling seascapes or enclosing mountain walls. She was a flatlander, and she reveled in it.

Or did she? For almost 48 hours Cassie had been unable to leave her farmhouse, unable to force her foot across the threshold, no matter how hard she tried. She couldn't understand it. She was a P.I. and she had work to do. Someone had shot an arrow into State Sen. Mortimer Mux's porcine back, gruesomely decapitated the obnoxious Ron Rassendeal, and tried to drown Ron's brother Rudy in the toxic cesspool of a nearby mega-hog farm. The press was filled with stories about murder, money and corruption in the Capitol. Were the stories connected? Was one hand responsible for creating so much mayhem? Cassie didn't feel like she was following so much as a single lead. She'd dispatched Sheafhecker to search for the Modulator, but it was she who had to get to the bottom of things. She was in charge. She had to go to Springfield; she had to GO!

Cassie touched her fingertips to the cold windowpane. She'd heard of pioneer women driven mad out here on the plains, poor immigrants from crowded homelands who wouldn't adapt to the wide open spaces, whose spirits were crushed by the great weight of sky pressing down from horizon to horizon. Was it happening to her? Had life on the vast plains finally taken its toll? Would she be trapped inside the farmhouse forever, a victim of creeping agoraphobia? Or worse, plain fear?

Clenching her fists, she turned to the front door. Cassie had to get moving. She had murders to investigate, corruption to expose, wrongs to right. She had to find the threads connecting casinos to mega-hog farms, for that thread, she knew, would lead her to the lair of a cold-hearted killer.

She strode determinedly to the front door, sighed and grasped the knob. She flung the door wide, took one step onto the porch, then reeled as if punched by a right cross. Stumbling inside, she slammed the door behind her. Dizzy and sick, scarcely able to stand on rubbery legs, she still felt a deep sense of satisfaction. It wasn't some weakness that kept her housebound. It wasn't agoraphobia, it was stinkophoibia!

The fumes from the neighboring mega-hog farm were potent enough to melt all-weather paint from a combine harvester. When the wind was right-- wrong, really-- no one could stand on her front porch for more than five minutes without losing every lunch she'd ever eaten.

Cassie swallowed hard and slowly straightened. She wiped the thin film of perspiration from her forehead and fixed her gaze on the laptop computer resting on her grandmother's rolltop desk. Why hadn't she thought of it sooner? Cassie might have been physically unable-- unwilling?-- to battle her way through the mega-hog farm's nauseating stench, but her spirit could still soar-- electronically.

Cassie sprinted across the living room and logged on to the computer. In the course of her work as a P.I. she'd established a network of informants, each of whom owed her favors. She clicked onto a screen icon and watched a window to her electronic mailbox open. It was busy.

The screen names-- carefully coded to confuse prying eyes-- rang a whole carillon of interesting bells. After retrieving and glancing at a few from contacts and her lawyer, Ostrogoth, she noticed an urgent message from Bonita Rassendeal. Bonita was the wife of Rhiny Rassendeal, so estranged from her late ex-fiance that he was a "non-Rassendeal," really. Bonita also was an ex-waitress at Pizza Mind, the favorite restaurant of Garth "Paisano" Jones, Toluca's crime kingpin.

Cassie had pounded Toluca's mean streets once upon a time, following the scent of a pair of militia-wannabes stealing fertilizer by the barrel, and she had picked up a few useful facts along the way. Bonita, Cassie knew, had provided Paisano Jones with something more than an extra shake of parmesan during her waitressing days there. Indeed, the waitress and the country-fried mobster had given the phrase "all-you-can-eat" a whole new meaning.

If Bonita's scurrilous, scandalous past ever came to light, it could cost her dearly, but her secrets were safe with Cassie. She would tell no one about the 11th and 12th "extra toppings" never printed on Pizza Mind's menu.

"Let's see what's up with Paisano Jones' bit of extra sauce," Cassie muttered, tapping the keyboard to open Bonita's message.

--Cassie! Are you there? Your phone's not picking up and

all hell's breaking loose. It's been awhile, I know, but I hope you get this before Paisano sends a few other body parts by airmail.--

Cassie sat up and took notice. "By airmail" could mean only one thing: Paisano Jones had catapulted Ron Rassendeal's head through Cassie's bedroom window. But why? She read on.

--I'm not talking about Ron's head.--

Cassie slumped.

--I'm talking about prime bits sawed off my husband's prize pig and sent here and to Senator Mortimer Mux in a sealed plastic baggie inside an envelope that the Unabomber would admire. This weekend Rhiny's pet pig was abducted and carved into pieces during a fair. Rhiny just got back home, crushed, and opened up the package and cried out when a cloven hoof from the Senator was there. The pig Senator, that is. The prize pig, that is. Then he noticed the severed ear-- the right one, with the rose, not the left one, that read Senator. Rhiney will never win another blue ribbon for studliest porker, and I'll never have another long weekend home alone until the next romance happens my way. And now Mux, as you must know, is dead.--

Cassie shook her head and leaned back. She couldn't understand why Paisano Jones would pull such a violent stunt on Rhiny. And why send pig bits to Mux? Her eyes returned to the screen.

--If you're wondering why Paisano's on such a tear, I'll tell you. After Rhiny retreated to the bedroom to grieve, I phoned Paisano, who laughed. He said someone snitched to him that all of the Rassendeal boys were in bed with Mux over this land-based casino deal. I told him that Rhiny's in the clear-- Rhiny hasn't spoken to either Ron or Rudy in years-- but when Paisano's on a rampage, he won't listen to reason. Not even

from me, who shared so much with him in so many ways for oh, so long. Over and over. Paisano is a primitive, a brute and a wonder in many ways, but I digress. He can be so frustrating! Paisano says that if anyone's going to open a casino not docked to some riverboat landing, it'll be him, not some fat senator and a few fake descendants of a little-known Indian tribe.--

Cassie rubbed her eyes. So Paisano had threatened Senator Mux. Had he engineered the senator's murder as well?

--My country & western Italian stallion swears he had nothing to do with Mux's murder, but I don't know whether to believe him or not. You remember how it is with Paisano and me. He's such a tough and I'm so weak and spineless. He's bad to the bone...

Brother, Cassie thought.

... But if this he hired someone else to do the dirty work, then technically he's in the clear. Paisano swears he never touched Ron Rassendeal's head, either, but that doesn't mean he didn't touch Ron's neck with an axe or something. He can be rough. And passionate. But not always pleasant.--

Cassie shuddered and glanced involuntarily over her shoulder. Paisano was a thug, but smart. She suspected he had some influence over grain elevators in a few central Illinois counties, and knew he had delusions of grandeur. The owner of Paisano Trucking hauled grain and gravel, coal and hogs. And in some places, according to the talk, he took cuts from the sale of farm implements, anhydrous ammonia deliveries, tankers of corn syrup and ethanol, and barge loads of tofu heading south to New Orleans and east to Asia.

But that was mostly just talk, Cassie thought. In his own mind, at least, Paisano influenced central Illinois agribusiness like New York gangsters influenced the docks in the bad ol' days. In fact, however, Jones had set up some intricate corporate structures, subsidiaries and shell companies, but his being the corn-and-beans godfather was limited. Paisano's scaling and skimming, kickbacks and protection rackets were safer and easier than running robberies or a farm checkoff system, but he wasn't a Wise Guy. But the talk in Toluca was that Paisano would like to move up to the Big Leagues, and he was making his operation seem more than penny ante to attract a merger offer.

Right, Cassie thought, like coyotes merge with kittens. Still, she eyed the computer screen nervously.

--It's not about greed with my snuff-dipping sophisticate, Cassie. It's about looking good. Saving face. If Paisano lets a casino open up on his patch of Earth, he'll be the laughingstock of the big shots who really run the Farm Federation, the "Grocery to the Globe" conglomerates, and the syndicate. No casino can open without his input-- and take-out.--

Logical, thought Cassie, but where does that leave me? If Paisano's pool room goons murdered Ron Rassendeal, mutilated Rhiny's prize pig, and shot an arrow into Senator Mux's back, what could she do about it? Bonita's message continued.

--Maybe you can find out more about the Pawsitees. I don't think Paisano cares if it's a supposedly extinct Indian tribe or the Rassendeals, whether there's mega-hog money or just political shenanigans. He won't let anyone muscle in on his territory without a fight. But I think he'll settle for a truce if his cut of the action is big enough. Is it possible to bring the sides together, Cassie? If not, I have a feeling no one between I-80 and I-70 is safe. Let me know what you find out. If you want, I'll do what I can to keep Paisano's mind on other business.--

"I'll bet you will," Cassie murmured. "Extra cheese, onions, and special sauce on the side."

Dusk had settled over the great plains. Cassie switched on the desk lamp and mulled over Bonita's frantic e-mail. How could she bring the sides together when she wasn't sure who they were? She knew about Paisano Jones, but the Pawsitees were a mystery. Her history books had one entry: "A tribe in the Illini nation." The libraries and museums were silent on the tribe. Only the town carried their name.

She got up to stretch her legs, wondering where Sam was, and wandering back to the window. As she stared into the gathering gloom she was nearly blinded by two glaring beams of light. Cassie squinted, but she wasn't startled. It looked like Red Pavlow, her taciturn partner. He must be using her tractor to spread nitrogen fertilizer on the field across the road, she thought.

Cassie was surprised Red hadn't checked back in with her on what the Ag Lab found out-- if anything-- about Roylott's pumpkin pie. She also had yet to politely ask him about Rudy and the lagoon swim. She'd have to call him...

Her hand flew to her forehead as a thrill of excitement traveled through her. Red! Of course! Red had Native American blood in his veins. His collection of arrowheads was second to none. He'd once mentioned learning about Illinois' vanished inhabitants from his elders and knowing more than a barnful of professional scholars. If anyone should be able to tell Cassie what she needed to know about the Pawsitees, Red could.

She darted over to the telephone, dialed Red's beeper, then returned to the window. A moment later, the machinery's headlights swerved and pointed straight at the farmhouse. In a few minutes, Cassie thought, Red would arrive, and she might have some of her answers.

Cassie opened the door, stepped onto the porch, put her

hands on her hips, took a deep breath, coughed once and smiled defiantly.

7

PRAIRIE DAWGS

Steven Burgauer

Not far from where Route 24 crosses the Mackinaw blacktop is a little patch of ground not unlike so many other similar patches of ground, except in one respect: a wonderful bar once stood there.

Nowadays, the building's just a burned-out shell of its former self, but back in the late '70s the Dew Drop Inn was a popular hangout. Folks from as far away as Bloomington and Peoria invariably came by as part of their regular Friday-night circuit. Everyone was welcome, of course, farmers and sodbusters and especially bikers-- so much so that it became almost like a clubhouse to the Prairie Dawgs, a tightly-knit fraternity of motorcycle riders. Now, once a year, just before Halloween, the old crowd gathers for a reunion.

Bikers are a funny lot, and not just because they don't fit in comfortably to any one, simple niche. They come from all walks of life, and are just as serious about their sport as, say, Corvette owners or Jeep enthusiasts. And though they sometimes look the part, they're not really rebels. Nor are they ruffians. Oh, some are, to be sure-- and they get all the headlines-- but nowadays, most of the Dawgs are just family men, with mortgages and kids of their own. One of their number-- Carl Lynn-- is even a cop, a sergeant with the Tazewell County Sheriff's Department. Another is the son of a local mayor. A third, an employee at a local hospital.

For the old gang, biking is now just one part of a larger picture called the "good old days," memories that grow fuzzier with each passing year.

And like any gathering of men who are just a little bit beyond their prime-- soldiers, athletes, bowlers-- the stories of the good-times-past grow richer and more fantastic with each telling. Thus, it should have come as no surprise to anyone that, when Franklin Peeves pulled up at the site of the old Dew Drop Inn, spewing out wild tales of having seen the White White Witch, no one believed him.

And who could blame them? Franklin was a spoiled brat, always had been. And as if that weren't enough to make him suspect, ever since his father-- Joel "Pet" Peeves-- was elected mayor of Peoria, Franklin had had a bit of a credibility problem. No sooner had he parked his hog and taken off his helmet, than he started in with his tale.

"I seen her," he said, breathless. "Not five minutes ago!"

Everyone was seated around a campfire enjoying the heat of the burning logs. There were six or seven of them, each clutching a bottle of beer. An ice chest sat within easy reach a few feet away. In keeping with tradition, the fire had been built exactly on the spot where the pool table once stood in the old bar. Their bikes were parked behind them, off to one side, over by where the bathrooms used to be. Though most of the Dawgs swore by their Harleys, the lineup included a Kawasaki and a Yamaha. Every once in a while you'd see a Greeves or a Bridgestone, but not tonight.

"I'm not kidding," Franklin said. "I seen her!"

"Who?"

"The Witch."

Carl laughed. Police from throughout central Illinois had been on the lookout for this girl for four years now. Seeing her was one thing, catching her another.

"I even got one of her leaflets," Franklin said, pulling folded paper from his pocket for all to see.

They read it by the flickering light of the fire. It was just like the ones they'd seen or heard about before. On it was written but a single word, in big bold type: REVENGE!

Peeves continued, "Followed her for about half a mile, I did. Then I lost her over by the Snodweavers' place. She's fast on that Harley. Damn fast!"

"They say she murdered ol' Mortimer Mux," one of the boys said, tossing another log on the fire. On the back of his jacket, in big gold letters, was printed his street name-- Digger. He used to work at the Springdale Cemetery before it got shut down.

"Man deserved to die if you ask me," Lucifer Matthewson chimed in. "Mux was a pig."

The bikers nodded. They respected Lucifer. He was a Matthewson, one of THE Matthewsons, from around Trivoli. His great-great-great Uncle Byron died in the Civil War, and had his name carved in stone on that monument in downtown Peoria.

"Doesn't sound like something a woman would do," Digger retorted.

"What the hell you know about women anyway, Digger?" Franklin said, looking down his nose at the other man. "You're on your third wife, aren't you?"

"What I meant was, shooting a man in the back with an

69

arrow, cutting off another man's head and putting it in that...
that pumpkin chucker, that takes a lot of stones. Just don't
sound like a woman to me."

"That's where you're wrong," Lucifer observed. "Women
got more range than us men, more breadth. The kind ones are
gentler; the evil ones, meaner. Still, the Rassendeals have ticked
off a lot of people over the years. The used-car business. Their
chain of mega-farms, what, Porklips? Why blame this rider?"

"Same goes for Mux," Digger said. "He's got more
enemies than Pet's got peeves."

"Leave my father out of this!"

"Or what?" Digger taunted. "You'll have your daddy come
by and give me a lecture on morality? Or send over one of his
crews to put up some speed bumps in my neighborhood?"

Those were fighting words, and Franklin balled up his fist
into a knot and bolted after Digger. He got in the first punch
before Digger knew what hit him. But it would also Franklin's
last punch, because he was no match for Digger McGrue.

They both fell to the ground, Digger pummeling Peeves.
But before he could do much damage, Lucifer pulled the
cemetery man off, and Carl stepped in to hold back Peeves.
Even at their age-- their early forties-- fighting remained a part
of the biker's code.

Wiping the blood from his split lip, Franklin said, "I think
she wants to be caught."

"What makes you say that?" Carl asked, loosening his grip
on Franklin's arm a bit.

"Used to be, she rode just once in a while. You know, July
4th, Labor Day, Halloween. Now the press says she's been out
riding every night. Reports are coming in from everywhere, you
said so yourself."

"So what kinda revenge you think she's looking for?" Digger asked.

"Who's to say? Maybe ol' Mortimer molested her."

"That's a real possibility," Carl agreed. He'd heard rumors about Mux.

"But then why's she riding around naked? Girl like that could catch her death."

Everyone laughed and the tension was broken. The cooler was opened, glass clinked on ice, and bottles were passed around.

"You know, though..." someone said, "she might be one of us."

A few sideways glances and everyone burst out laughing. The alcohol was beginning to speak.

"No, what I mean is-- she's a biker. Maybe she's from the old club. You know, the Prairie Dawgs."

Franklin's explanation was greeted with skepticism, and groans were heard from all around. Back in the days before the bar burned to the ground, back in the days when they were all still a lot younger, the Dawgs had been a biker's club. It had numbered about 24 in its heyday-- boys and girls alike-- and they rode all over Tazewell and Woodford counties harassing their neighbors. Now there were only about six or seven of them left for these annual get-togethers.

"I see what you mean, Peeves," Digger said. "But if that's the case, it's got to be a pretty short list. There's only about three or four of them gals that fit the bill. 'Less, of course, Betty lost a lot of weight."

Chuckles again, this time followed by catcalls and a loud "Moo."

"Now wait a minute," Franklin said. "Don't be so quick to

laugh. This gal's outsmarted every cop in the county, including you, Carl. If we catch her, there might even be a reward. My daddy says the Rev. Roylott of that Deferred Judgment Church came by his office a while back asking for money, money to help track down this Witch. Wanted to hire that lady detective, Cassie Canine."

"Kuh-NINE, not Kay-nine," one of the drunker ones said. "Anyway, what do you need a reward for? Your family's loaded."

"Oh, shut up!" Franklin turned and snapped, almost losing his balance. "Daddy's got the money, not me. Anyhow... he sent the preacher packing and Kuh-NINE had to settle for whatever Roylott and his people raised going door to door. But... I'll bet you... if Roylott and those fanatics he calls a church can afford to hire Kuh-NINE, they can afford to spring for a reward. My Daddy says... "

"Your daddy, hell," Digger said. "If he plays his cards right, he'll be able to step right into Mux's seat in the statehouse. Election's next month and everyone knows your daddy's not happy just being mayor."

Franklin nodded his head and blinked twice but didn't reply. His father's ambitions were no secret, really. Known as the "Speed Bump Mayor," Peeves' political career had more speed than bumps.

True, "Pet" Peeves had become embarrassed by the town that elected him mayor. The river was brown, and everyone knows what else is brown. And there were cows, actual cows, grazing in the fields just outside of town! And God knows, those cows are what might have made the river brown to begin with! And there wasn't a Bible on every school desk or a basketball hoop alongside every driveway, and the city councilmen never did their homework...

However, there were those dog-gone speed bumps to slow down cars. A TV network picked up a local report on the traffic-control gimmick one night, the Chicago **Herald-News** and a wire service had followed suit, and now Mayor Peeves was a household name throughout the state. Ashamed of Peoria or not, he'd become a favorite to be appointed to finish the term for Mux's district, which included parts of Tazewell and Peoria Counties.

Lucifer intruded upon Franklin's thoughts. "Before they put out a bounty on that sweet girl, they'll probably first come up with a reward for any information leading to the arrest and conviction of Rassendeal's killer. You know, like Cat did with those jackrock incidents."

"What does Cat know?" Digger said, finishing a beer and swiping foam from his lips. "If Porklips keeps expanding its megahog farms, Cat'll be the laughingstock of the Fortune 500. Can't you see the headlines in the **Wall Street Journal**? 'Cat HQ Waist Deep in The Big Stinky,' or 'Dividends Down as Cat Cleans up own House'."

At first there was an explosion of laughter. Then Carl cleared his throat and sobered, becoming a cop once more. "There's your motive, boys."

"For killing Mux?"

"And Rassendeal."

"Just how many beers have you had, Carl?"

"Forget Mux already, and Rassendeal too," Franklin interrupted, shaking his head. "I know which way the Witch was headed when I lost her. If we put our heads together, we ought to be able to track her down."

"Yeah, as if you were still sober enough to drive."

"I don't mean tonight, fool. I mean tomorrow. There are seven of us, right? If she's riding every night now, we can stake her out tomorrow night."

"Peeves is right," Carl said. "We got a map down at the station house with every sighting flagged on it. If we stake out a few key intersections between Pawsitee and Pekin, Morton and the river, and keep in touch with cell phones we might to be able to get her."

"It's settled then," someone shouted, and they all clinked their bottles with drunken gusto. "Long Live the Prairie Dawgs!"

•

She cored the apple with surgical precision, the circular tool glinting under the bright kitchen lights.

Each time the sharpened tool took another victim, it rang hollowly against the wooden cutting board. Peel and seeds dropped carelessly to the floor. Apple juice sprayed across the counter, making her hands slippery. Blood dripped from a spot where she'd nicked herself earlier.

The moon sagged against the horizon, making her kitchen window a mirror against the night. The woman looked at herself in the reflection and smiled. She was naked. Next to her on the floor was a stack of leaflets. Each one read the same: REVENGE! After what happened last night in Springfield, another ride seemed dangerous. But exciting.

Missy hated Mux. And it wasn't just his politics. Mux might be-- might have been-- amoral. Without a moral compass or gyroscope. Lacking in values, or beliefs, or faith. He might even have been evil, she thought, suddenly coring another apple with a satisfying thud.

But now she was a suspect; that is, the White White Witch was. Even worse, she had no alibi, and police were already out looking for her. The cop that caught her was sure to get a promotion.

But it got worse. It had already been in the papers that the Rev. Roylott and his Council of Concerned Citizens had been out raising money to hire that detective, Cassie Canine, to track her down. On the other hand, one story featured a kid named Sheafhecker who Canine had set about snooping around, and he seemed like a dunce. This probably was a good omen. For whatever else Missy thought of Canine, the woman seemed to be making only a half-hearted attempt to find her.

Missy laughed; she couldn't help herself. But it was a kind of wicked laugh. The sort a witch might make. Missy was no witch, of course-- though that's what the media called her-- and certainly not a warlock like her old biker buddy friend Lucifer Matthewson. No, Missy was just an ordinary country girl. An ordinary country girl with a lot of pent-up anger. And tonight she had almost been caught. By one of her own, no less. She wondered whether Franklin had recognized her.

Missy shook her head. If he had, the police would already be here. Her secret was still safe. But for how long?

Missy reached into her sink and pulled out another apple. A dozen or more were still floating there in the water, getting clean.

She reached for her tool.

Whomp!

Seeds and juice flew everywhere. A tiny chunk landed on her cheek, next to her mouth. A fleck of appleskin was still attached.

She reached out for it with her tongue and urged it past her expectant lips. The tiny morsel slid down her throat and brought tears of joy to her eyes.

Gosh, she thought, it was great to be alive!

8
GET YOUR
MOTOR RUNNING

Joel Steinfeldt

"Take thy banner! and if e'er
Thou shouldst pass the soldier's bier,
And the muffled drum should beat
To the tread of mournful feet,
Then this crimson flag shall be
Martial cloak and shroud for thee.
The warrior took that banner proud
And it was his martial cloak and shroud."

-- Henry Wadsworth Longfellow
"Hymn of the Moravian Nuns of Bethlehem,"
inspired by General Casmir Pulaski's Legion,
which rode into battle against the British with a silk banner
embroidered by sisters at a convent in Bethlehem, Penn.

Missy scraped the apple slices into the potpourri crock with her knife, inhaling the steam from the herbs she grew in the garden behind her house just outside Goofy Ridge.

She bent to scratch the only inky spot on her white, white cat.

"I got your belly, Blackjack," she said as he eyed her

clownishly, sprawled near her leaflets, pink pads in the air.

She spent her days alone, making the occasional dirt angel at night in desolate soybean fields, staring at Andromeda. When the thunderstorms rumbled in she would play her old eight-track, dancing in the kitchen with Blackjack in her arms.

Until IT became part of her like the white scar on her left hip, dried brown blood on her mattress and the gold ring of her great-great grandfather in her pierced navel.

Missy was a radon baby.

She grew up like many Illinois River valley teen-agers in the early Cat-depression '80s, listening to southern rock and smoking Marlboros in her friends' slightly radioactive basement bedrooms as the earth exhaled the fumes of the uranium deposited by the same glaciers that covered the land with black earth.

Her body had always been her best weapon.

She didn't realize it until her tight tube-top, hip-hugger blue jeans and 17-year-old brown-eyed boldness got her arms around Digger McGrue's chest and her boots on the pegs near his Harley's exhaust as it grumbled into the cemetery just outside Pekin.

They lay, unknowingly, behind Sen. Everett Dirksen's tomb, drinking Wild Turkey and listening to the Allman Brothers on the older man's boom box as Digger buried his face into her brunette curls.

And when Dickie Betts got to the finish of "Tied to the Whipping Post" to close radio's "King Biscuit Flower Power Hour," she asked Digger for a motorcycle of her own. He bought her a used Harley Superglide the next day.

But eventually, she left him for Jesse Matthewson, the one called Lucifer. And there were the bikers who survived the bar stabbings, overdoses and whiskey-soaked, late-night 120 mph jumps over California Road Hill. They had no names or faces. She rode them like the white ponies she galloped on as a girl on the steam-powered merry-go-round the old farmer always brought to Manito's annual Popcorn Festival. Until IT happened.

One Sunday she rode past Pawsitee's three bars, and on a whim, killed the motorcycle's motor outside one of its two churches.

She fell in love while he delivered his sermon. His face was still flushed with the exertion of speaking as they flirted briefly at the narthex door as he bid parishioners farewell.

Sitting in the first row at the service the next week, her riding leathers discarded for her only Sunday dress, she almost dropped the note she found slipped into the fourth chapter of Job as she opened the pew Bible. There was only the name of a Peoria bar on it.

She went there that night, and in a back room near midnight she saw him preach again. But this time it was a Liza Minelli's "Cabaret," his face barely recognizable under the cheap red lipstick and bad black wig as he delivered his "sermon," into the eyes of his associate pastor, who cheered from the front row.

He had sat next to her in the pew.

Missy rode home and sulked, guzzling Jim Beam and flipping sullenly through the Pekin paper. When she read that Pulaski Community Academy in Chicago and 21 other schools had filed for permission from the state to let students attend school on the first Monday of March, the whiskey, the "sermon" and the ponies all crashed into her like the cannon shot that crushed her great-great-grandfather Oct. 15, 1779, outside Savannah. She was crushed. But IT made things worse.

The last of a lost weekend extended for days-- until she

heard a radio news story about a local politician's fund raiser. She blinked and tried to shower away her pain and grief and dread. Her shock. Missy thought she'd appeal for help for her heritage-- for Illinois' own history-- if not for her own personal state.

Then IT happened, shocking her, soiling her, demeaning her like no biker ever had. Afterward, weakly, Missy nursed her Harley home, where she drank and stripped, drank more and smashed dishes, eight-tracks and the bathroom mirror, the shards ripping a red mouth into her hip.

When she awoke, her hair had turned platinum. All of it. Everywhere. She didn't see Blackjack for days.

"Never forget you carry the blood of a hero," her grandfather had said, before the Pall Malls ate his lungs and left him like a scarecrow in his hospital bed.

They were forgetting.

She would not.

She drank off another hangover, rode to Peoria, pierced her navel and got her tattoo. Back home, she printed some leaflets on her MacIntosh and set out naked April 1, her bottom burning as she roared into Sand Ridge, the state forest in northern Mason County.

The tires on Zophar, her black, black Harley, easily handled the sandy soil of the hiking trails. She could appear anywhere north, south or east of the forest and disappear swiftly, leaving only a trail of leaflets to turn mushy in the morning dew.

Though the occasional bug that made it past Zophar's windscreen brought tears to her eyes at first, she learned to take pleasure from the occasional wet sting on the nipple.

If Peeves really wanted a "San Francisco of the Midwest" he at least ought to open a nude beach and begin an aerial mosquito spraying program, she thought. He already had the gay bars.

Since then, Missy never rode on The Day. And while she loathed Mux-- he repeatedly introduced bills to rescind Public Act 80-621, but they died in committee-- she wondered, would Peeves, Mux's likely successor, do the same?

It mattered less to her when she rode. Tonight Zophar had vanished beneath her, and instead she charged on a moaning chrome horse down blacktop roads through rows of yellowing corn into the harvest moon that seemed to rest on Goofy Ridge.

Missy rubbed Blackjack's belly again and inhaled the steamy essence of apples. After so long. Revenge. Sweet as apples. Yes, Missy thought, she would need to ride again-- tomorrow night.

●

Cassie saw the combine's halogen lights as she pulled her car past the Indian mound at the entrance of the long driveway that led to her farmhouse.

"What in Sam Hill is Red doing spreading fertilizer this late?" she wondered aloud, stopping to get out.

But wait-- that was Sheafecker's machine. She could hear the combine's blades turning as it came in a slow circle toward her.

"Sam!" she yelled, walking forward to meet him. "Sam?"

She stumbled on a corn stalk stub and fell forward, nostrils filling with the scent of the black, wet earth. Lifting her head, she saw the tire patterns in her car's headlights. The harvester had circled repeatedly, the apex of the curve changing a few yards each pass.

She worked out where the pattern would take it-- toward the porch of her house, or maybe the mound. But now it was headed straight at her, lights blinding her as it rumbled closer. She gasped and stumbled to the side, avoiding the black knobby tires as it ground past.

There was no one in the lighted cab.

The blades had sprayed her with a mist of fluid as the combine passed, flecking her face and clothing. Cassie wiped a speck from her cheek with a finger, then dotted it on her tongue. It wasn't hydraulic fluid or oil-- it had a salty taste and a gritty texture.

Cassie waited for the combine to return. A black, wet stain in the housing behind the blades in its metal mouth shined for a second in her car's headlights.

She trotted parallel to it, her tiny frame dwarfed by the giant harvester, gauging its speed-- maybe 5 mph, but not so fast a sprint couldn't get her to the metal footstep below the cab door. She ran for a few seconds just outside the giant rear wheels, then darted sideways.

Lunging, she grabbed the handbar and hung for a moment between the tires, legs swinging, the harvester's engine roaring in her ears.

A clump of dirt thrown from the front wheel hit her in the mouth, and she gasped again, spat, and hung on. Cursing, she put her heel in the footstep, leaned back, and turned the door hatch.

Cassie scrambled into the driver's seat and grabbed the wheel, turning it only slightly before the rope tied between the spokes to the base of the seat stopped it.

"The ignition," she thought, grabbing for the key. There was only a empty hole. Beneath the dash was a tangled mess of wires.

"Hot-wired," she said aloud. Glancing up through the

windshield, her eyes watered from the bright lights. Her car!

She whipped the wheel right as far as it would turn, missing the car but slamming into the earthen wall of the mound.

The impact threw her ribs into the wheel. Gritting her teeth, the combine shaking as it tried to surge forward, she ripped wires from under the dash until she heard the engine sputter, then die.

Cassie sat panting, looking around the cabin. Sam's coat hung from a hook next to her. She searched the pockets, finding only a Polaroid of a footprint-- a big one-- and a piece of pumpkin shell.

Headlights flashed on the side window of the combine. It was Red.

"For crissakes, Cassie, what the hell have you been doing with Sam's combine?" he asked, stepping from his truck, peering at her with a flashlight in his hand. She climbed down and told him.

"I'm O.K.," she told the worried man as he took it all in.

"What did the Ag Lab find? Did the pie match the shard? Why didn't you call me?"

"They laughed at me, Cassie," Red said. "They said you can't match pie fillin' with shell."

"Red, even the lack of a clue can be one," she said. She looked down, disappointed. One side of the mound had collapsed, the earth spilling toward the road. A leather bag stuck out from the pile. White bones and a necklace of tiny shells and bright stones glittered in the glow of Red's flashlight. She bent to pick them up.

"Leave them be," Red said.

"I just..."

"Leave them be."

"Why Red, I know you have Potawatomie blood, but...," she blurted before he cut her off.

"The soil you see isn't ordinary soil-- it's the dust of the blood, flesh, bones of my ancestors... You'll have to dig deep before you can find nature's earth. The upper part is my people. The land, as it is, is my blood, my dead; it's consecrated..."

"Who said that?" she asked.

"I don't remember. A chief, maybe. Or... it doesn't matter," Red said. "But I don't mess with the dead."

"We need to talk about your ancestors," she said.

"Yeah, but not now. We got to find Sam. Whoever hot-wired the combine must have jumped him. They could have just taken his key, ya know."

They traced the combine's tracks, walking in circles, Red's flashlight starting to dim. When Red stumbled in the field ruts, his boots making an audible squish, they found Sam. At least, most of what the combine's blades had left of him.

There were the usual phone calls, the blue and white flashing lights, the coroner with his black plastic bags, another interview with Sgt. Lynn, and much later, Maggie Lynch, leading the media that the radio scanner traffic brought.

"We need to talk," she'd said. "A drink sometime? I'm in and out of the Capitol press room 18 hours a day. There are plenty of places to talk within walking distance."

Hugging herself as a wrecker moved into position to tow the combine from the mound, Cassie nodded and said, "Later."

It was very late, and more than her ribs ached. She had always felt guilty that it seemed like someone had to die before she could begin her real detective work, bringing the hunt, the tingling adrenaline rush she was addicted to.

But it had never been someone this close.

9

MORRIS
THE EXPLAINER

Joseph Flynn

As the dust settled behind Red's truck heading north, Cassie's head began to spin. And not just from the relentless smog of pig dung from the Rassendeals' PNI. There was way too much going on: decapitation, capitol murder, lascivious clergymen, movie parodies, and on and on. And she was at the middle of it all. She knew if she couldn't distance herself from this mess, get some sense of perspective, not only would she fail to solve any mysteries, she'd soon be on the bus to the funny farm... the loony bin... the laughing academy...

When the thought of life in a rubber room actually started to seem a little comforting, she grabbed her car keys and headed off into the autumnal darkness. As she pulled out and headed north to I-155, then I-74, she didn't know where she was going... Chicago, maybe. She had $700 of untapped credit on her Visa card; plenty of gas. Why not? Hmm, she thought. Odometer's got more miles than I thought. The car needs an oil change.

She needed an escape, a lost weekend. Maybe when the fog cleared she'd be able to make some sense of what was going on. She saw the Interstate signs for Chicago but changed her mind and swung onto the access loop for I-55 South. St. Louis. The Arch. The blues clubs. If she was lucky, a high time on a riverboat.

Springfield was en route. Maybe Maggie Lynch. The young reporter seemed less shallow than other journalists she'd met. Sharp, even.

Cassie settled into the right-hand lane of the southbound interstate doing a steady 70 mph. Speeding. But just barely. Fast enough to make good time to the big city, but not so fast a state cop would chase her down. There. See. She'd just zipped past the bumblebee brown and yellow of an Illinois State Police patrol car lurking on a highway entrance ramp, and the trooper stayed right where he was.

She giggled. Maybe he'd have shown a little more interest if she rode around like the White White Witch: buck naked! Or... or maybe, as scrawny as she was these days, he wouldn't have batted an eye.

And if Cassie and the Witch had both passed by the cop *aux naturelles* she had no doubt which one of them he'd pursue. Maybe she ought to be grateful that sniveling dweeb Rice Roylott considered her attractive. She found this thought so depressing it killed off all desire to reach St. Louis. Or anywhere else.

By the time she reached the Railsplitter rest area a few miles north of Springfield, she pulled off the road.

With a heavy heart, a full bladder, and a bad yen for sugar, she plodded into the rest facility. A map on the wall pointed out her location and said: *You are here.*

"Right," Cassie muttered. "But where do I want to be? That's the question."

She stepped into the ladies' room and when she came out

she saw Ed Asner emerge from the men's room.

He saw her, too, and knew immediately what Cassie was thinking. "No, I'm not him," the man said, "and if you ask me how Mary's doing I might *plotz.*"

Cassie didn't know what it meant to *plotz,* but she was pretty sure she didn't want to see anybody do it. Besides, another guy followed the man who wasn't Ed Asner out of the gent's room and Cassie immediately forgot about every other male in the world.

He was *gorgeous.* Tall and lean. Dark hair swept back in a dramatic widow's peak. A flawless olive complexion out of which shone brilliant blue eyes. And he was smiling at her. Not pushing it, just giving her an easy little grin that hinted at gleaming white teeth and secrets the two of them shared intuitively.

"Take it easy, O'Shea," said the man who wasn't Ed Asner. "You'll make her swoon."

Cassie swung her eyes to him and thought she might like to see him *plotz* after all.

The man laughed at her, but with good humor. "I'm Morris Mandelbaum. Your heartthrob over there is Jose O'Shea." Mandelbaum walked over to a vending machine. "I feel like having a chocolate bar. Can I get anything for you, Miss?"

If the two of them were together, Cassie thought it wouldn't be a good idea to cop an attitude with Mandelbaum, and she was hungry for sugar. "Um, sure. I'd like a Crunch bar, please."

"Joe?" Mandelbaum asked.

"Nothing for me, thanks."

"Of course not," Mandelbaum replied to his companion, feeding coins into the machine. "God forbid you should get a cavity or a zit."

Mandelbaum's words sent a chill down Cassie's spine. Here she was with the most divine man she'd ever seen, and she knew that with her first bite of chocolate every tooth in her head would fall out and her skin would break out all the way down to her toes.

"Here you go," Mandelbaum said, handing her the candy bar.

Then he sat down on a wooden bench, gestured for her to take the place next to him and said, "Sit. Eat, eat. You're as thin as--"

"Your margin for error when it comes to talking to strangers, Morris," O'Shea told Mandelbaum. He sat on the bench, too, looking Cassie straight in the eye, but leaving enough room for her to sit between them.

That was when Cassie noticed a suspicious bulge beneath Jose O'Shea's jacket. She looked around and saw they were the only three people in the rest facility, and nobody was pulling up outside. She thought what she ought to do was say thanks for the candy and make a bee-line for her car. But as she examined O'Shea's baby blues she couldn't find any menace in them. Not for her.

She sat between the two men.

"He worries about me," Mandelbaum told Cassie, "it's his job. So, what's your name, sweetheart?"

She told him. Morris asked her to spell that last name for him. Cassie did, through clenched teeth.

"Oy!" Morris Mandelbaum winced.

"Morris, stop," O'Shea warned.

"Look at her," Mandelbaum continued, paying his partner no heed. He took Cassie's chin and turned her face toward O'Shea. "She's a nice-looking girl. Too skinny but nice looking.

And her name, it couldn't be any worse if she called herself Betty Bow-wow."

"Now, wait just a minute!" Cassie shouted, leaping to her feet.

"Feeling a little defensive, sweetheart?" Mandelbaum asked innocently.

"You're going to tell her about Ida, aren't you, Morris?" O'Shea asked.

Mandelbaum nodded emphatically.

"Miss Canine," O'Shea intervened, pronouncing Cassie's surname properly, "I wouldn't blame you if you left right now."

In fact, it looked to Cassie as if he was silently pleading with her to go.

Which warmed her heart so greatly she sat right back down -- and made sure her thigh touched O'Shea's.

Morris Mandelbaum began his story: "When I was a young man, I had the great good fortune of being the son of my community's matchmaker. I knew I never needed to worry about the woman I would marry. I was sure my mother would pick the most beautiful, loving, altogether wonderful girl in the world for her only son to marry."

A beatific smile crossed Mandelbaum's face at the memory he'd conjured.

"And she did?" Cassie asked, interested despite herself.

"And she did," Mandelbaum agreed.

Jose O'Shea sighed.

Cassie gave him a cross look, for the first time feeling more sympathetic to the Ed Asner look-alike than the matinee idol. She ignored O'Shea when he gave a small shake of his head.

"What happened?" Cassie asked.

"On my 21st birthday, my mother introduced me to Ida.

Just as I'd always imagined, she was a vision of loveliness. Long, dark, wavy hair, the face of angel, a figure to inspire poetry."

"Only problem, her name was Ida *Lipschitz*," O'Shea added in the bored tone of a man who's heard a story more than once too often.

"Lipschitz?" Cassie asked Mandelbaum.

He nodded sadly.

O'Shea snorted in disgust. "Yeah, and Morris could never get past her name. Even after this perfectly nice--"

"Beautiful," Mandelbaum corrected.

"Even after this *beautiful* girl not only refused to take offense at Morris's idiocy but also said she'd gladly change her name to Mandelbaum once they got married."

"How could we get married without a courtship first?" Mandelbaum demanded of O'Shea. "And how could I court a girl named... well, you know. I mean, I was hoping for lips of wine, not lips of... well, you know."

"I warned you," O'Shea told Cassie.

"Now, undoubtedly Ida found someone else to marry," Mandelbaum continued. "Perhaps some poor fellow who was deaf and placed less importance on the spoken word."

"Oy!" said O'Shea.

Mandelbaum ignored him and went on. "But she didn't marry me, and we could have been so perfect together."

"Excuse me," O'Shea said. "I think my dinner's backing up on me."

He got up and headed back into the men's room. As Mandelbaum watched him go, a sly look came into his eyes.

"You don't have to make any decisions right now," he told Cassie, "but I've got some other names for you. Ones I think might turn your life around."

"How do you know anything's wrong with my life?" Cassie demanded.

Mandelbaum spread his hands in a gesture of appeasement. "Pardon me. It's just been my experience that most young women who have things figured out don't spend their evenings in highway rest stops talking to strangers."

Cassie gnashed her teeth.

"It's okay," Mandelbaum consoled. "I'm not exactly having gefilte fish at the Ritz myself, am I? Why don't you tell me what's wrong? I'm usually pretty good at helping people sort out their problems."

Morris Mandelbaum gave Cassie Canine a warm smile and made her feel just like Mary Richards sitting down for a heart-to-heart with Lou Grant-- and pour her heart out she did. And kept on pouring even when Jose O'Shea returned and gave Mandelbaum a look that would have scared the gonads off a brass monkey.

When Cassie finished, Mandelbaum nodded sagely and said, "Okay, I've got a couple things for you to consider -- other than changing your name."

"Morris," O'Shea growled in a tone that raised the hair on Cassie's neck.

"I appreciate your concern, Joe," Mandelbaum said in a calm voice. "But it is *my* tushie that's on the line, and I don't think this young lady is a threat. So sit down and let me speak."

Cassie looked from one man to the other, and, again, felt it more compelling to look at Mandelbaum.

He told her, "My full name is Morris 'The Explainer' Mandelbaum. Does that mean anything to you?"

Cassie shook her head.

"He's the guy who writes the endings for 90 percent of all mystery novels," O'Shea said, sitting down.

"Ninety-*nine* percent," Morris asserted. "What happens is these best-selling hotshots dream up their *ferkokte* plots, get everybody in all sorts of trouble, and then can't come up with the solution. So they call on me to make sense of everything at the end. I *explain* things."

"And since truth is stranger than fiction," O'Shea elaborated, "Morris explains to the federal government a lot of real mysteries that a lot of very bad people would rather leave unsolved. That's why he's in the Witness Protection Program."

"I'm afraid I have some real *momsers* after me. That's why Joe looks out for me."

"You're a federal marshal?" Cassie asked O'Shea.

He nodded tightly.

She thought that made O'Shea sexier than ever.

"Joe and I stay on the move," Morris said. "On the road. We drive between New York and Los Angeles a lot-- a lot on old Route 66 from Chicago south and west. We see a lot. Think a lot."

She turned back to The Explainer to hear his thoughts, his couple of things he had for her to consider.

"They're both about this *goniff*, Ron Rassendeal."

"What about him?"

"He's not dead. Most likely."

"What!" Cassie exclaimed. She started to say more, but Morris held up his hand.

"Wait. Before you say I'm *meshugge*, let me tell you a story. There was this fellow out in Oxnard, Cal. He had a thing for the wife of a dentist at his country club. Wasn't exactly subtle about it, either. Got so obnoxious the dentist had to slug him at a country club dance. The *putz* picked himself up but before he stormed out, he promised-- in front of a roomful of witnesses-- that he'd have both his vengeance and the dentist's wife."

Cassie hung on every word, and even O'Shea, who knew the story by heart, paid close attention.

"Six months later, the dentist and his wife were at home asleep in bed when they heard someone breaking in. It was the madman who hadn't been seen since that night at the country club dance. Luckily, at the wife's insistence, the dentist had bought a gun. Bang! The maniac was shot and killed. Everything worked out all right."

"Except?" Cassie asked.

"Except," Morris said, "the husband was dead, not the boyfriend. The boyfriend -- also a dentist, by the way -- spent three of those months he was missing having extensive plastic surgery to make him look just like the husband. Then he and the treacherous wife drugged the husband and using the same corrupt surgeon they'd brought up from Tijuana transformed the husband's appearance into that of the boyfriend -- the boyfriend who'd threatened an act of violence. So when the husband's surgical bruising disappeared and he looked just like the boyfriend used to, they set him up to make it look like he broke into his own house and shot him."

Cassie gave a low whistle. Then she had an insight. "And they knew they could get away with it because the boyfriend took over the husband's practice and nobody was the wiser."

"Very good," Morris nodded in appreciation. "So how were they caught?"

Cassie thought. "Somebody had to see something that was unchanged, something private. Oh, my! The husband had a lover the wife and the boyfriend didn't know about, and she surprised the impostor somehow."

"Very sharp indeed," O'Shea complimented Cassie. "She caught him in the shower."

"Now, for you, seeing a head come flying through your window must have been very shocking indeed. I doubt whether you or anyone else stopped to look for signs of cosmetic surgery, but if you go back and examine the remains, I bet you find your victim isn't who you think he is."

Cassie was thunderstruck. She wanted to race out and put her hands on that bogus head right now... but she remembered that Mandelbaum said he had one more thing to tell her.

"That name: Rassendeal. It's worse than Lipschitz. Can't possibly be real."

"What is it if not a real name?" Cassie wanted to know.

"An anagram. That's what a lot of wiseacres do when they want to disguise their true purpose and have their little joke at the same time. So what's an anagram for Rassendeal?'"

Cassie thought feverishly. "S-A-N-D-A-L S-E-E-R?"

"Or S-A-L-A-D S-N-E-E-R," O'Shea guessed.

"Maybe S-A-N-D L-E-A-S-E-R," Cassie suggested.

Morris "The Explainer" Mandelbaum shook his head. "With all those pig-poop pools you have bothering you, I think it's probably E-R-A-S-E-S L-A-N-D. As in despoils the environment. I could be wrong-- it's happened once or twice before-- but I think you're dealing with an ingenious eco-terrorist here. He's so smart that, other than the occasional homicide, he's found a way to muck up the environment with the very food you eat."

"Then there's no way to save ourselves from Porklips Now, Inc.?" Cassie asked, stricken.

"You could declare your county kosher," Mandelbaum offered.

"Have everybody go vegan," O'Shea suggested.

Cassie frowned. She knew that people in Central Illinois would never give up their bacon, pork chops and ham. Still, she was energized, too. She had to get going. Maybe she would share some ideas with Lynch, get a fresh point of view.

She gave Morris "The Explainer" Mandelbaum and U.S. Marshal Jose O'Shea quick kisses-- okay, O'Shea's lasted a little longer-- and ran to her car, thinking she might change her name to, say, Tracy Hepburn.

The two men watched her drive away.

"You could have explained the whole thing to her, couldn't you, Morris?"

"Sure, Joe. The whole schmeer. But where's the fun in that? Besides, even if they don't give me credit, you know I'll have to come back to pick up all the *tchatchkes* littering this story."

O'Shea laughed. "Come on, Morris. Let's get out of here before somebody else comes along and you tell them what happened to Jimmy Hoffa."

"You worry too much, Joe," said Morris "The Explainer" Mandelbaum.

10
EXTRA-CELLULAR
COMMUNICATIONS

Terry Bibo

"Well that's about enough of that," Cassie snorts as she strides down the walk to her car.

Snapping blue eyes and square shoulders notwithstanding, it is time to get practical. She'd dumped a fiancee over pigs, she can get her mind back on the mysteries at hand. Cassie Canine, P.I., is not normally one to bat her eyes, giggle, and stand about while the pig dung is flung. Having that ex-fiancee's head come flying through her window set her back a bit. Now it is time to move.

She wraps her slender fingers around the cracked car door handle and yanks it back. Most days, that is the only way to get in. Today it chunks her in the shoulder and she yips a bit in pain.

Damn this thing, she thinks.

She gets in, belts up, cranks the key.

Nothing.

Damn it to hell, she thinks.

Just as she smacks the steering wheel with the palm of her hand, the car phone rings. This is a surprise, since Cassie leaves the mobile phone turned off unless she is using it. Cassie

97

operates under the novel assumption there should be some place where one is not subject to the electronic whimperings of the world and the front seat of a moving vehicle is as good as any.

"Canine," she barks.

"Who?" says a tentative female voice.

"Who did you call?" Cassie snarls.

"I-- I don't know," the woman stammers.

"What do you mean you don't know?" sniffs Cassie.

"I found this number in his pocket..."

"In whose pocket?" Cassie interrupts.

Some might think this rude, but rudeness had gotten Cassie a long way. Contrariwise, rudeness had also kept her from going too far down the wrong path with an obvious loser on more than one occasion. For example, the late Ron Rassendeal.

"He was riding on a combine. I told Paisano he didn't mean nothing to me," the woman whines. "I think his name was Sam..."

Cassie bites back a tart reply. Like a well-oiled roulette wheel, her mind spins, clicks and holds. She grabs the phone so tightly that her knucklebones shine out clear as an X-ray.

"Bonita?" she guesses. "What do you know about Sam?"

"I know he didn't want to cook on my kitchen table," the woman says dully. "And when I checked his pants pocket to see if he meant it, I found this piece of paper... Hey, is that you, Cassie?"

"Of course it's me," Cassie snaps. "How did you get ahold of Sam's pants?"

"Oh, he was still in 'em," Bonita says. "We never got much farther than that. He was in too big of a hurry. But I kept this number, just in case. I didn't know it was yours. And now I got to warn him."

"No," Cassie says. "You don't."

The phone is silent. For a moment, Cassie thinks Bonita has hung up.

"Sam is dead," Cassie says finally.

That gets a reaction. Bonita squeals in fear.

"Oh, Cassie, you've got to come up here," she sniffles. "I can't do this by myself any more. Sam's dead and Ron's dead and Rhiney's pig is showing up one chop at a time. And I think I know why."

"Why?" growls Cassie, hoping rudeness will save her a trip to the estranged Rassendeals' farm in rural McLean County.

"I can't tell you over the car phone," Bonita says in a suddenly hushed voice. "You'll have to come here."

"I can't," Cassie says. "I'm on my way to Springfield to meet somebody."

"After," whispers Bonita. "I don't care when you get here. Just get here."

This time, when the phone is silent, Bonita really has hung up.

Cassie flips her phone shut and pitches it on the passenger seat. She cranks the key and the unpredictable little VW engine buzzes to tinny life. Never again will I buy a vehicle made in Mexico, Cassie vows. When they made Volkswagens in the U.S. you could count on them. Now I'd be better off with a burro.

She pretends the car is reliable, which is the best she can do, and sets its nose toward the southbound highway. It is time to find out why there are more dead bodies in Tazewell County than there are Apostolic Christians. That means follow the money, she thinks, and if you follow the money you're bound to end up in Springfield.

Squid Pro Quo

Twenty minutes later Cassie pulls up in front of the State Capitol building. Twenty minutes after that, she's found a parking spot. And 20 minutes after that, she's hiked back to the *Herald-Star* office under an Easter Island head of steam. Maggie Lynch had better be good.

She is.

"Cassie Canine," Maggie says, sticking her hand out for a shake. "We ought to make quite a pair. We've got men dropping at our feet. Or their heads, anyway, in your case."

Stalking around the stacks of old newspaper clippings and press releases, she pops the door of a small refrigerator tucked beside a battered desk.

"Beer?" she says, proffering a sweaty Sam Adams.

"I thought this was your office," Cassie says.

"You don't work here as a statehouse reporter, you live here," Maggie says. "Most of the best stuff happens before 9 or after 5."

She slides open the desk drawer to reveal a pair of pantyhose, three Tampax, a can of tuna, a can opener, four packets of Earl Grey tea, and a small white cardboard box.

"Straight pins, bobby pins and safety pins," she says, cracking the lid so Cassie can get a look. "Not to mention $8.47 in change for the vending machines. Sometimes even Domino's won't deliver."

Cassie is impressed.

"I guess if Mortimer Mux had to get shot in front of anyone, he was lucky it was you," she says. "I'm surprised you didn't give him CPR and write down his last words at the same time."

"I tried," Maggie says shortly.

The would-be Lois Lane is still very young, and her journalist's skin is still very thin. Even a three-decade police reporter would have trouble with an arrow-struck man bleeding at her feet. The fact that the man was a porcine and repulsive public official trying to feel her up while impersonating Abe Lincoln would only make her feel worse. Objectivity demands she cover her loathing by trying to find something likeable about the guy. The beaver hat, maybe?

Cassie cuts to the chase, sketching out the details for the reporter who'd become part of the story.

"Do you think there is some connection between all these murders?" she asks.

"Gee whiz," Maggie snorts, revived by the chance to be sarcastic.

She ticked off facts on her fingertips.

"Here's what I've been told: Your ex-boyfriend's head is shot through your window by the now-missing Q36 Aludium Pumpkin Modulator. Your would-be brother-in-law shows up at your door covered with pig poop and says he was fighting with him over the family business-- whether to bring hogs to the slaughter in a mega-farm or hicks to the slaughter in an Indian casino. Your legislator is shot with an arrow that probably came from your partner's collection. Your minister, who has the hots for you and whose wife just died, takes the time between services to bake you a pie that may or may not have been made with parts of the pumpkin your ex-boyfriend's head was wrapped in. One of your boys is run over after hunting down some clues for you on his combine. Your would-be sister-in-law keeps offering you mysterious clues. And your would-be brother-in-law that nobody wanted to talk about has his champion pig swiped and chopped and mailed back to him..."

She stopped this breathless recitation for a dramatic flourish, "Do you see any connection here?"

"Me," Cassie says almost inaudibly.

"Well, that's one," Maggie says. "The obvious one. But there's another."

"Money," Cassie says more firmly.

"Absolutely," Maggie says. "And when you figure out who's got it, who's getting it, and who's losing it, you'll find out who's got reasons to kill."

They sit in silence for a moment. Maggie sucks on her beer absent-mindedly.

"You know," she says. "Mux's widow is probably going to run for his seat. Between his campaign war chest, his insurance and whatever other boxes of money he's got laying around, she ought to be able to buy herself a permanent job.

"Makes me think," Maggie continues. "How close were you and Ron? Before PNI?"

"Pretty close," Cassie says tightly. "We would have been married by now."

"Close as your family farm and Porklips Now?" Maggie probes. "Close enough to know how PNI was set up? Close enough for him to put you on, say, his insurance policy? Estate close?"

Practical though she may be, Cassie clearly has not thought of this. Did Ron take her out of his will when she broke off their engagement? The Rassendeals owned PNI, right? But who was CEO and so on? And where did Rudy get that box full of money? Did he have to take it out of Ron's house before it was turned over to... to whom? Mux, sure, but originally Cassie? Or the Department of Ag? Rudy said he was going to put the casino by the hog farm. But the property next to the hog farm was now

Cassie's place... Or, like Morris said, was Ron even dead?

And if she WAS his beneficiary, did this mean she could shut down the hog farm, quit the P.I. business and buy herself a new car?

Cassie shook herself. That was cold. She looked up to Maggie's narrow-eyed gaze. Rookie though she may be, Maggie is shrewd enough to read more of Cassie's thoughts than she might like. Cassie kicks the refrigerator door. Time to throw this woman off track.

"How about a beer?" she says.

On Golden Pond

Later, hiking back to her car, Cassie's anger-- and most of her energy-- have drained away. She isn't looking forward to the drive north to McLean County.

She yanks on the car door. It hits her smack in the center of the sore spot from the last time. Damn car, she thinks automatically, but there is no venom behind it.

Cassie clambers into the VW and straps her seatbelt across her birdlike frame. She fumbles for the key, wiggles it into the ignition and turns. Nothing.

"God damn this car to hell," she mutters.

On the seat next to Cassie, the little phone tinkles. Apparently, there is no such thing as normal any more. She scrambles for the gray plastic and flips it open.

"Cassie Canine," she says.

"How are you doing, Cassie?" trills a high-pitched, yet vaguely familiar voice.

"Just fine," she replies, wondering how her number got so popular, but too tired to interrogate.

"It's Greta, honey," says the voice. "Greta Alexander."

Greta Alexander was a housewife known to few outside her family until she was hit by lightning that bolted through the wiring in her television set during a freak storm. In the decades since, she'd become famed for her open-hearted giving, her folksy advice and her psychic ability to find things. Sometimes she found lost keys. Sometimes she found dead bodies. And all the time she has lived in tiny historic Delavan, not 15 minutes from Cassie's farm.

"How did you know where to find me?" Cassie says.

"Think about it, Sweetie," Greta says.

Cassie does, but not for long. Greta sounds like she looks-- Aunt Bea on steroids. It's actually rather soothing, despite the sometimes gruesome bits of data fetched from the netherworld by her "angels."

"Never mind," Cassie says. "What can I help you with?"

"Nothing, hon," Greta says. "It's what I can help you with."

"OK, I'll play," Cassie groans. "What can you help me with?"

"A few bodies," Greta says. "At least one, maybe two or three. You know, local people hardly ever call me about these things. Most of my murder calls come from out of state. It's not like we don't have enough mysterious deaths around here, especially lately."

"That's for sure," Cassie says. "Just take your pick."

"I think I'll start with Ronnie," Greta giggles, just one of the extra-large extra-sensory girls. "Your ex."

"Was that Ronnie's head?" Cassie asks.

"Stay local, sweetie," Greta says. "Of course it was. But the real question isn't the head. It's the body. How come nobody asks what happened to the rest of him?"

"What did?"

"I don't get road maps, kid," Greta says a trifle testily. "Just impressions. And when I think of Ronnie, it's hard to see."

"Then why did you bring this up?" Cassie snaps, a trifle testy herself.

"I didn't say I couldn't see anything. I said it was hard to see. It's dark. And it's heavy. It's warm and it's thick, like soup. It smells. It's strong. It's getting stronger. And Ronnie is not alone, or he won't be for long."

"What does THAT mean?" Cassie yelped.

"My angels say the Indians' Great Spirit knows the answer to that," Greta says.

"Red did not have anything to do with this," Cassie snaps.

"Then my angels say your troubles are all behind you now," Greta intones.

"Well, my angels tell me that I ought to quit listening to fortune tellers and get on with it," Cassie says.

"OK, hon," Greta says, all sudden cheer. "I never tell anybody what to do. But I promise you'll remember what Greta said."

The line, again, goes dead.

Cassie snaps the phone shut and pitches it aside, this time being extra-careful to turn it off. With that same extra-precise motion of a very tired or very drunk person, she fits the key into the ignition. The VW roars to life, a burro pretending to be a racehorse, and she jerkily backs out of the parking spot.

In the neon-green light of the dash, Cassie's eye catches a rounded shape toppling aside in her back seat. She doesn't remember putting anything back there, so she turns to examine it more closely. She thinks she has seen something like this before, not long ago, and it wasn't pleasant.

It wasn't.
It was another head.

11
OFF
THE BEATEN PATH

Garry Moore

Imagine having a conversation with someone on your car phone and then turning around to see their head in the back seat.

What would you do?

For Cassie Canine-- sleuth-turned-ball-of-nerves-- the answer was simple. Upon seeing a head, Cassie felt at once feverish and chilled. Upon noticing Delavan psychic Greta Alexander, Cassie fainted.

However, she didn't lose consciousness before the shock caused her to jerk back, putting her car into Drive, its pedal to the metal. She may have been out like a light, but her car was in motion.

She didn't see the ducks, hear their clucks, witness an old man's agility, pay for his spilled groceries, or heed the cries from a few bystanders out late in downtown Springfield.

Instead, Cassie was racing, lead-footed, away from the Capitol with reckless abandon, as stunned pedestrians and motorists held their collective breath.

●

With the exception of Morris, maybe, few could explain

how Greta could talk to her **while** decapitated, Cassie thought. That was Greta... always full of surprises. Her existence in parallel universes was the stuff of legend. In the years to follow, she may be missed, but not before solving more mysteries. It could take folks a while to realize that Greta was channeling in her predictions from afar...

●

Red also sensed that something was wrong. Like Greta, he also was connected to the spirit world. (Cassie hadn't called him when she said she would.) But his motivation for speeding off the farm had more to do with uninvited guests than finding his boss.

Paisano Jones had come calling on the Canine farm with a couple of henchmen, it seemed.

Red had spotted a fast-moving car making its way up the county blacktop, and with all arrows increasingly pointing toward him as a chief murder suspect, he wasn't about to roll out the red carpet. When the car turned onto the dusty entrance to the farm, Red saw that Paisano sat in the back seat, beside a couple of silhouettes.

Hurriedly climbing into his pickup, Red glanced over his shoulder and noticed that one of the shadowy figures was a Toluca waitress he'd seen years ago. Whatever Paisano's motivation, it turned sharply suspicious as the other figure, driving-- a strange black man he knew as Wienie-- spotted Red and turned the wheel his way.

In the car, Paisano said, "Follow that car."

"Yes suh, boss," smarted Wienie.

●

Back in Springfield, Greta's head continued to shout metaphysical messages to Cassie in an effort to revive her. False alarms that she was "about to hit the Governor!" or "Watch out for that lobbyist!" didn't work. Only "You've got to find out who murdered Sam" awakened her, and not a moment too soon. Eyes opened quickly to see a Mack truck... blur... wrong way... swerve... old lady, sidewalk, storefront, customers, Lotto sign, vegetables, firewood in plastic, pumpkins, airbags, and on, and on...

Greta may not have been full-bodied, but her head proved potent enough in its ability to lead Cassie to a prime source; for this was no ordinary Springfield storefront. This was Mux Produce Deluxe, one of the late Senator's properties. Now, thanks to this accidental find, it was caved in. Bricks, plaster, shingles, two-by-fours and produce-- mainly pumpkins-- buried Cassie's car. Luckily, no passersby were injured, but Cassie thought the situation looked grim for her-- and Greta.

When rescue workers arrived in a swirling haze of fog and flashing red lights, the accident scene was roped off. Authorities told the reporters who suddenly appeared-- including a wide-eyed Maggie Lynch-- that it would take hours before they'd be able to unearth the occupants.

As Cassie overheard a frustrated paramedic say, "We need something to scoop up these damn pumpkins and get 'em the heck outta here," she began to feel funny. Claustrophobic, maybe.

But in back-- beneath a pile of bricks and pumpkins in her cluttered back seat-- Greta (er, her head) murmured, "You need the Aludium Q36 Pumpkin Modulator, hon'!"

•

Wienie, the driver, had a hard time keeping up with Red. The Lexus belonging to Paisano was nearing 90 miles per hour, but the sleek sedan wasn't gaining any ground on the old pick-up. (Years ago, Red had done some work for John Bearce.)

The old truck really picked up speed after Red turned onto I-155, and headed south.

Presumably for Springfield, thought Paisano, who said, "This might work out."

Bonita Rassendeal, somewhat hysterical-- an improvement for her-- sniffed and said, "What?"

"Don't lose him," Paisano said to Wienie, adding, "Aw, what the hell, we got business ahead anyway."

●

Wienie had been in his share of chases before. As he stared at the tiny taillights of the old pick-up ahead, his mind flashed back to his Black Panther days in the early '70s. He remembered how his group would pursue members of street gangs, hoping to recruit them for the more wholesome involvement of Revolution. That was before the CIA dropped drugs in his community and he became hooked on heroin, and a shell of his former self.

On the streets, he'd paint his face red (in honor of Native Americans, he'd say sometimes) and live off the land, sometimes making meals of street animals. Somewhere in there, back there, he befriended members of a white motorcycle gang (a logical match, notwithstanding Woodstock). One member was special to him: Missy. He taught her how to hunt cats, skin squirrels, appreciate her body, get arrested for shelter purposes, live unnoticed in former slave quarters in homes on Moss Avenue, and seek revenge.

Then one day-- like his breath on any given hour-- their relationship soured. They'd just finished debating the Patty Hearst story when he said something about how Casimir Pulaski

Day was an attempt to trivialize Martin Luther King Day.

Missy stormed out of his place, taking her Joan of Arc posters.

"Goodbye, Mr. Young-- if that's your real name!" she shouted, mumbling hints that any future visits would be nothing less than acts of terrorism. And they were. She'd ride her motorcycle through his cardboard street dwellings, phone in false reports about him to newspaper columnists, and call P.A.W.S. before he had a chance to capture his prey.

He was reduced to roadkill cuisine.

But Wienie would survive. He'd gradually escape her street vandalism and torment, and after a bad experience at a Kids Nowadays festival-- someone mistook him for Ronald McDonald-- he cleaned up and persevered and eventually, recently, found a job.

It wasn't until a day ago, however, that he found out that he worked for a gangster. Kind of.

Wienie planned to quit today, but now found himself part of what seemed like some sort of strong-arm squad.

The least of his worries was that he'd get a speeding ticket, but out of habit he glanced at his rear-view mirror. He saw something that made him sweat. It was the light of a motorcycle. Gaining on him.

•

Sgt. Carl Lynn left the McDonald's in Morton and thought about rousting the group of migrant workers gathered on Jefferson Street.

"Just what are they up to at this hour?" he pondered, looking at them and his watch and back. "Law's still on the books."

Instead, he started up his standard cop car-- a Chevrolet Caprice Classic sedan-- and drove past one strip mall toward another, well-manicured lawns lying tidy around well-maintained homes housing well-ordered lives everywhere he looked.

Lynn sighed and absently drove south of Morton toward Pekin, past Pawsitee, and had thought about getting back to Morton to question those migrant workers. So he slowed to turn onto the ramp for northbound I-155 to head back.

Then he heard it.

Like a giant fly being zipped. It came from the Interstate. He'd heard that sound before. It was a speeder. He pulled to a stop and straightened his cap.

Then he heard it again; another zip.

Then a third.

He peered over the concrete railing of the overpass to see the blurring taillight of the last vehicle. Debris blew in its trail. Leaflets?

Intuitively, he knew. It was her.

Carl grabbed his two-way radio, then froze.

He put the microphone back in its dashboard cradle and picked up his cell phone.

"Digger, it's me. Carl. Tell the boys I'm on the White White Witch."

Within minutes, Digger notified the core of the Prairie Dawgs. A couple of them lived between Pawsitee and Lincoln-- a good position to intercept the White White Witch if she was indeed "heading down I-155 toward Springfield," as Carl indicated.

●

A pie expert, the Rev. Rice Roylott wanted only the best pumpkins to make the scores of pies and Jack O' Lanterns he traditionally gave out each year to needy families. At least, that's what he told people each year, when he put on the Big Beg at the Libby's plant in Morton. Each year, reluctant company exec's let the good Reverend drive a Libby truck (filled with pumpkins) off the factory lot after the second shift ended. Paternalistically, Rev. Roylott would tip the migrant workers, whose job it was to load the truck. And tonight, they'd spent their money eating at McDonald's and looking over the the empty indoor playground.

Rumor had it that the Reverend would NOT donate ALL of the pumpkins; that he had some business partner somewhere who'd warehouse the bulk of the pumpkins for the purpose of selling them. Such rumors often were spread by people with axes to grind; folks like Rudy Rassendeal, who tonight may have been seeking to prove that theory by following the good Reverend. Or maybe Rudy was just confused.

Regardless, with the Libby's truck and Rassendeal's car passing west of Lincoln as I-155 dumps into I-55-- which expands to three lanes each way-- Rudy was feeling light-headed, satisfied with himself for using such information to build a broader coalition for his casino project.

But thoughts of extortion, money and power all evaporated like sweat off his brow when the procession passed.

First came an old pickup, a motorcycle close behind, overtaking it. (Geez! Rudy thought. Was that that hired hand's?) After those two vehicles, a nice Lexus knifed by, then a cop car -- its lights not blinking despite all of their speeds. After an interval of almost a minute, a few other motorcycles zipped past.

Rassendeal twitched with recognition and dread. He shook his head. It didn't clear, but the Libby's truck still ahead of him.

As all the vehicles headed to Springfield, each party's motivation remained a mystery.

12

PORKLIPS NOCTURNE

Tracy Knight

With the suddenness of a cymbal crash, Cassie erupted into consciousness.

It seemed days, or even decades, had passed.

Mercury vapor light bathed the interior of her car, casting a sickly bruising glow across everything: shards of windshield glass, decimated vegetables, the moist meat of pulverized pumpkins. She pulled her coat tightly around her; the chill night wind whistling through the car's broken windows was growing fangs.

The driver's door opened suddenly, all but spilling Cassie to the ground. A dark figure reached in, grabbed her left forearm. The disoriented Cassie wondered if she were being abducted by an alien. After witnessing the disembodied, jabbering head of Greta Alexander, it seemed consistent with whatever membrane of reality she had ruptured.

The figure was clad entirely in black and wore a tightly fitting helmet with a smoked, impenetrable visor.

A muffled voice from within the helmet: "Come with me. Now."

Cassie passively acceded, letting herself be pulled from the car. If the figure had not held her up, her dizziness would have prevented her from standing upright.

Absently looking around, Cassie observed blurring silhouettes talking and pointing to her car and making unintelligible comments to one another. None seemed to notice, or to care, that she was being abducted by an alien.

The figure leaned closer, until the visor pressed against Cassie's left cheek. "I've talked to the police. They'll question you later. They know where to find you."

After a sharp intake of breath, Cassie coughed several times. A wheeze whistled up from the deepest caverns of her lungs. Sweat trickled down her forehead and into her eyes. Finding her voice, she said, "The back seat... there's a head. It was talking."

The dark figure strayed from its lumber-stiff posture, head tipping to one side like a puppy bewitched by a firefly. It released Cassie's arm and quickly leaned into the car, emerging with...

A pumpkin. With a long dark wig secured to it.

"I thought that it was Greta Alexander's head," was all Cassie could manage.

The figure laughed, handing the pumpkin to Cassie. "Don't tell Greta."

Seizing Cassie's arm again, the figure tugged her toward the black Harley-Davidson that sat at the corner. "Get on."

The feverish Cassie possessed neither the orientation nor the will to resist. Cradling the bewigged pumpkin, she managed to swing one leg over the sloping seat, waited for the black figure to climb on in front of her, then clamped her free arm around the figure's midriff.

The smooth thrum of the motorcycle as it buzzed down Wabash must have tempted Cassie back into unconsciousness,

for the next thing she knew the motorcycle had stopped in front
of a smallish pub. A shamrock-emblazoned sign announced it as
The Barrelhead.

Cassie struggled off the Harley, then stood there wavering
against the rising force of the icy midnight breeze.

The figure reached up and slowly removed its helmet.

Long nova-white hair pulled free, cascading down across
black-leathered shoulders.

"It's... you," Cassie whispered.

A wide smile creased the beautiful face. "Happy to meet
you. You've been looking for me. My name's Missy. I think
you know me as the White White Witch."

•

Wienie took a Downtown Springfield exit off I-55, letting
the Lexus's tires squeal so sweetly they might have been playing
an old blues tune.

"Please, make him slow down," Bonita purred, rubbing her
cheek up and down against Paisano's shoulder. "Your delicate
kitten might melt with fear, my gorgeous Don Juan de McLean."

A tiny chuckle escaped Paisano's lips. "If you melt, see that
you don't stain my white slacks."

Sensing that her well-practiced kittenesque act wasn't
playing, Bonita sat up straight. "Honey, are you sure you want
to do this? Don't you think it's dangerous?"

Paisano shrugged. "Perhaps it is, but don't you feel it,
Bonita? The rush of adrenaline, the hot blood pulsing through
your veins, sharpening your vision, clearing your mind, filling
you with life?"

"I guess so," she lied, disappointed that she was missing out
on a borderline erotic experience. "But, Paisano, aren't we

117

talking kidnapping here?"

"In a way. But it's just a reporter. It's not like most people would give a wedge of head cheese if a young journalist disappeared off the face of the earth."

•

Both the ambience and the patrons of the Barrelhead were half-lit. Cassie and Missy settled at a corner table, Missy promptly ordering them each a vodka tonic, a bowl of chili, and a slice of apple pie.

"Feeling better?" Missy asked.

"I think so. But I still feel weird. Hard to concentrate. Hard to breathe."

"Something's wrong. You're not a fainter. And you've got sores on your hands," Missy said, pointing. "One more bad thing happens to you, your life will qualify as a country-western song."

Cassie scrutinized the two angry-looking, weeping red sores, one on each palm.

"Stigmata," Missy said, then snickered. "Martyrdom's in your future."

"The pumpkin. The wig. What was that all about?"

Retrieving the pumpkin from the floor, Missy peeled off the wig, then removed a piece of paper hidden inside its crown. "I can't tell you what it's all about, but I *can* tell you who put it there."

"Who?"

"The only person I know who owns a wig like that. I buy an occasional wig at the same boutique."

"Who is she?"

Missy laughed, a tad too enthusiastically. "Not a she. A *he*.

A pastor, to be specific."

"You mean. . .? Noooooo."

Missy nodded. "Rice Roylott. I thought I loved him once, thought he might be the gleaming light to shepherd me out of the grotto of vacuous existence. But he shunned me, made me feel as out of place as a Mennonite in a mosh pit."

Resisting the urge to delve into Rice's cross-dressing, Cassie asked, "Why would he leave that in my car?"

"It's just a guess, but I've learned to trust my instincts. Listen: I know he loved you, and he left the wigged pumpkin in your car either to save you... or to threaten you."

Missy took the paper she'd found inside the wig and gingerly flattened it on the table. Seeing the word REVENGE on one side, she said, "I can't believe he used one of my leaflets. He has more guts than a slaughterhouse." She turned it over and Cassie noticed a block of text on the other side.

"Let me see that," Cassie said, pulling the paper close. It was a short paragraph about *pfiesteria piscicida*, the aquatic, highly mutable "cell from hell" that had been discovered in hog factory waste. Symptoms of exposure to it included lesions, fatigue, numbness, difficulty breathing, and the inability to think and reason.

"Who knows," Missy said, "maybe it's mutated into a unique element-- Dinglebarium-- capable of producing shouting-head hallucinations."

"Why would Rice want me to know this?"

"It's a REVENGE leaflet; he's either telling you the pfiesteria is a vehicle of revenge being visited on you... or he's trying to warn you, inviting you to exact your *own* revenge."

●

The moment the throbbing red lights appeared in the rearview mirror, Red sighed deeply and pulled his trusty truck to the shoulder of I-55. He was done, he decided. It was over.

Red rolled down the window, listening to the approaching footsteps.

"Sorry, Red," Carl Lynn said, shining a flashlight in Red's face. "You gotta come with me."

"Why?"

"You're under arrest for suspicion of murder."

Resigned, Red unlatched his lap belt and exited the truck, kicking gravel as he shambled to the cruiser.

Carl smiled sympathetically. "I know you, Red, and I wouldn't have figured you as a killer."

"Who do you think I killed?"

"Ron Rassendeal," Carl said, then haltingly read his cheat sheet of Miranda rights.

"I didn't kill anybody," Red muttered, "but. . ."

"What?"

"I came upon Ron's body after he'd been murdered. I imagine you can find the body in the PNI waste lagoon."

"Why didn't you tell anybody?"

Red shrugged. "For what he's done to me, to Cassie, to everyone, I defiled him, separated his spirit and his body to wander isolated from each other into eternity. He deserved at least that."

"You beheaded him?"

Red nodded, gulped. "Spiritual tradition."

"And shot his head through Cassie Canine's window?"

Red laughed weakly. "No way, Carl. Whoever hurled the head had bad aim."

Carl chuckled and gave Red a playful punch to the arm.

Then the laughter died.

•

"It's almost closing time," Missy said, patting away a few bean flecks from her cheek. "We need to be moving. I'll get you home."

Cassie smiled. Missy's prescription of alcohol, chili and apple pie had left her surprisingly rejuvenated. Only a whisper of dizziness remained as testament to how ill she'd been.

Once outside, Missy said, "We can't take the Harley. Too many people looking for me. Besides, I'm done with it. I'm ready to turn the page to the next chapter of my life. Crazy no more. I've been crazy, too, believe me." She sighed. "Crazy no more."

They walked two blocks to a used car lot with flapping plastic pennants encircling it. Without hesitation, Missy hopped the fence, broke the side window of a red Honda Civic with her elbow, crept inside and hotwired it, all within a span of two minutes.

She drove the Honda through the flimsy fence, pulled up next to Cassie.

Getting in, Cassie felt obligated to say, "This is car theft, you know."

Missy jammed the stick shift into first gear and spun gravel, tires screeching all the way to the Dirksen Parkway. "That was a small satellite of Rudy's used car empire. So you see: It wasn't car theft. Just a remarkably good Rassen-Deal!"

Soon they were on I-55, heading toward Peoria.

Missy said, "You mentioned Greta Alexander. Did you ever talk to her, I mean in real life?"

Cassie nodded. "From what she said, I suspect there's

121

important evidence hiding in PNI's waste lagoon. Maybe even a body."

"Yes!" Missy shouted. "That's right!"

"How do you know?"

"I learned an approach to problem-solving from an old man once, a guy I met at a rest stop."

"Morris the Explainer?" Cassie said, disbelieving.

"Morris the *Befuddler*, he told me," Missy said, "but far from befuddling me, he bequeathed me the gift of lexical divination. Answers are magically hidden within words. Listen: Scramble the letters of PORKLIPS NOW, INCORPORATED (PNI), and you know what you get? WIN CORPSE! PLOP IN ROT, PARD! OINK! See? See how clear it all becomes? There *is* a corpse in the 'rot,' the waste lagoon. Oink!

●

"Oh, my," murmured Bonita, gazing upon the wreckage of Cassie's car. "I surely hope she wasn't hurt."

"Pipe down," growled Paisano. "It's after midnight and there's still much to do. We're not here to do an accident investigation. We're interested. . . in that!"

He pointed toward Maggie Lynch, who stood next to the ruined car busily taking notes.

They waited silently in the car until Maggie had completed her note-taking and began walking away, along the nearly deserted street.

Paisano instructed Wienie to follow her carefully with headlights off, giving him strict orders on what to do once they were abreast of her.

Wienie pulled up next to Maggie, threw the Lexus into Park and leapt from the car.

In a whirl of motion, Wienie dashed to her and grabbed her around the waist, simultaneously clapping one hand over her mouth. She struggled valiantly, her flailing arms nearly knocking loose the dead sparrow stapled to the brim of his hat.

Wienie dragged her to the car and shoved her into the back seat, where Paisano situated the young reporter between himself and Bonita.

"Don't be afraid," Paisano said nonchalantly.

"I know you," Maggie said, her voice quavering. "You're Paisano Jones. You're some kind of mob kingpin. "

Bonita giggled. Patting Maggie on the shoulder, she said. "Don't worry, dear, we're not going to kill you, oh no. *Au contraire...*"

Paisano rolled his eyes.

". . .we're going to give you an exclusive."

Puzzled, Maggie turned toward Paisano.

From the inside pocket of his suit coat he plucked out a small wallet. Flipping it open, he displayed a shiny golden star. "Does this look like something a mob kingpin would carry?"

Maggie pulled it from his grasp and looked closely. "You're a state agent?"

"A renegade agent, but an agent just the same," Paisano said, tightening his tie proudly and protruding his lower lip with the tingling enthusiasm of a testosterone-inflated Barney Fife.

●

"We're all insane," Missy said. "Some of us express it creatively, energetically, even poetically. Me, for example. Others express it quietly but, ultimately, more pathologically. PNI, for example. "

They were halfway home. Cassie had let the obvious questions rest long enough. "Why ride around stark naked, tossing REVENGE leaflets? Poetic madness?" She let the question drift in the air between them, not pushing.

Missy cleared her throat before replying, "That chapter of madness was born when I went to visit a man who could've restored my family name, Pulaski."

"Like the holiday?"

"Exactly. I went to see him after a fundraiser at Pawsitee Town Hall to discuss legislation. He had me in his RV. 'Had me' in every way you can imagine. Used and discarded me. Now it's right. The work is done, the play is over, the fake Lincoln is dead. Revenge. Relief."

"Wait. Are you saying—?"

"Wearing Indian garb and the black wig that reminded me of Rice."

"Wait!" Cassie said. "Don't tell me any more." She touched Missy's forearm. "Please. I don't want to know."

Missy smiled. "You *are* a friend. So I'll tell you this: My... pursuit of justice extended beyond Mux's perfect death and the celebratory ride I took the next night. Once I found out Rice Roylott was entwined with PNI, I decided to exact revenge, but not through action; through knowledge, finding out everything I could about them."

Cassie realized that no matter how much ground-level P.I. work she'd done on this case, a strange, white-haired Rough Rider was now helping her put the pieces together. She felt relief, and not a small bit of gratitude, even though she was troubled by the confession Missy had *almost* delivered.

Missy continued, "The Good Reverend's wife's lingering illness would have wiped him out financially. That's why it was important for him to have a financial benefactor."

"PNI?"

"Yeah. All he had to do was their bidding."

"What did that include?"

"I'm not sure, but I'm convinced they used his infatuation for you to get him to make contact, to get you in his good graces, within his grasp."

Cassie flashed back to Roylott's impromptu pumpkin pie delivery and shuddered. "To what end?"

"To get your land. Trust me on this. I'm a witch in the best sense of the word. Conjuring is a matter of paying attention, focusing, thinking, feeling. Living."

Silence swelled within the car for a few moments. Then, as they crossed the Tazewell County line, Missy said, "The more I learned about the mega-hog farms, the sicker I became. You know they keep the pigs so tightly confined they can barely move during their six months of life? And do you know what that causes? Psychologists call it 'learned helplessness.' Once the pigs realize they have no options, they lie down, quit struggling, go into a depression. They give up. Maybe there's more depression among humans because we're all eating depression-saturated pork chops. And maybe PNI is banking on its neighbors reacting just like those pigs: lying down, thinking we have no options, just letting it happen, giving up. People assume that Midwesterners are fatalistic by nature."

"You think that's true?" Cassie asked.

Missy shrugged. "True or not, there's nothing we can do about it." She let loose the most beautifully wicked laugh.

●

Red tied the last knot tight in the rope encircling Carl's

wrists.

"You sure you want to do this?" Carl asked sheepishly. "Gonna get you in a lot of trouble."

It was difficult to sound authoritative while standing in a ditch next to the Interstate. Half naked.

Red steadied the revolver he'd taken from Carl as he jammed Carl's pants beneath his arm.

"The way you talk, my friend, I'm already in a lot of trouble."

Red cocked his arm and threw the keys to Carl's cruiser over a wire fence into a field of stubble.

Carl said, "You're not the man I thought you were. I can't believe you're doing this to me."

"I'm not sure I know any of us," Red said, nodding, wondering at that moment if his ancestors' spirits were looking down upon him with pride or shame. "But look at it this way, Carl. You've still got your head."

Red eased into his truck, shot a U through an "Authorized Vehicles Only" trail, and headed north.

"See you around," Carl called, his eyes wandering down to his white white legs.

●

Back at Cassie's house, Missy tended to her like a loving sister: bringing her water to drink and spreading warm washcloths across her forehead. "You're sick and you've had a full night," Missy said. "It's 3:30 in the morning. Sleep. Tomorrow we'll act."

Cassie drifted into sleep with a smile on her face and didn't awaken until after sundown the next day-- October 30, Halloween Eve-- when the phone rang.

Missy walked into the bedroom. "It's Alaric Ostrogoth," she said. "He says he's your lawyer."

After the long sleep, Cassie felt healthy, refreshed, almost shimmering. She picked up the bedside phone and the moment she said hello, Alaric started bellowing. He was a sweet man, but didn't seem to have the ability to moderate the volume of his voice. It was always stuck at 10.

"Cassie?!"

She held the phone three inches from her ear, the proper distance from which to have a conversation with Alaric. "Yes?"

"I'm happy to hear you're there! I thought you'd have been arrested for Ron Rassendeal's murder by now!"

"Me? Why?"

"Why?! Who could have a better motive?! I'm not the estate planner here, but I happen to know that you're the sole beneficiary of Ron's estate!"

"Which means...?"

"Which means, my dear, you'll have a controlling interest in Porklips Now, Incorporated!"

Cassie felt her jaw drop. Then, even as Alaric continued to bellow, she hung up.

She looked up to Missy, who stood in the doorway. "He told me--"

"I know what he told you. I could hear." Missy fingered her lip thoughtfully. "Fate is summoning us. You know what we should do? Sneak into PNI, let you take a good look at what you're inheriting. If you plan to fight Hell, you need to know the geography."

●

As the stolen Honda Civic approached PNI, the first thing

Cassie noticed was that someone had defaced the spotlit billboard marking the mega-hog farm's entrance.

The billboard sported the figure of a cartoon pig-- Hamilton "Ham" Forquer, the Happy Hog-- holding a steaming breaded tenderloin in his pudgy right hand, a curious nod to cannibalism. Before, the cartoon had been framed with the words PORKLIPS NOW, INC.: TREAT YOURSELF TO THE BEST!

Recently, someone with both a sense of humor and well-developed artistic acumen had perfectly altered the painted text to read PORKLIPS NOW, INCORPORATED: EAT YOURSELF TO DEATH!

Cassie and Missy shook with laughter as Cassie pulled the Civic into PNI's main drive.

Missy said, "Laughter. The perfect psychic vaccination before inspecting a mega-hog farm."

"I hope no one's here," Cassie said.

"Not a chance," said Missy. "Trust me. These places run almost automatically. They check the pigs three times a day, tops. The Ebs check out the pigs, the Mr. Douglases rake in the cash, and the Mr. Haneys lobby the legislature. If there's anyone here but us at 11 p.m. at night, it'd be as surprising as getting a pearl necklace out of a Vend-A-Bait machine."

Missy hopped out of the car, jimmied open the locked gate, and motioned Cassie to enter.

The two drove slowly over the winding asphalt roads of PNI, marveling at the number of large pole buildings where pigs were housed.

"It's a regular Bradley University out here," Cassie said.

"Or Auschwitz."

Cassie pulled up next to one of the metal pole buildings and shut off the car. The two walked to a side door, already wincing against the dense odor that layered itself around their faces.

Cassie pulled aside the large sliding door. "Let's check in here,"

"You're the owner," said Missy.

Cassie nearly pitched backward with the stench. And it wasn't merely the stench of manure.

"Good God," Cassie said, pressing her hand over her nose and mouth.

There wasn't one squeal from the hundreds of pigs cramped in the building, and for good reason.

Although the building was still full of pigs, they were-- each and every one of them-- dead.

"Something's gone terribly wrong here," Missy said.

"Let's go home," Cassie said. "I've seen enough."

"Wait! Look!" Missy gestured excitedly toward the distant entrance.

Headlights. Someone was coming.

"Let's get out of here," Cassie said as she entered the car.

"What are they going to do, kill us?" Missy said. She considered what she'd uttered, nodded and slid into the passenger seat.

The mystery car was in the distance but there wasn't any doubt; it was coming their way. Fast.

Cassie started the car, backed up and, keeping her headlights off, pulled around the back of the building, toward the very rear of the PNI complex.

"I'll find a secluded spot and hide," Cassie whispered. "Maybe they'll leave."

"Don't bet on it," Missy said.

No sooner had the last word left Missy's mouth than directly behind them, two headlights blazed.

The clap of a gunshot. The whiz of a bullet ripping through the air.

Cassie slammed the accelerator to the floor, propelling both of them flat against their seat-backs. At the edge of the building, Cassie cornered hard, the back of the Civic fishtailing out of control momentarily before she brought it under control.

She glanced to the rearview mirror. "Dammit!"

The car was still behind them, gaining.

Without headlights, and now too engaged in driving to turn them on, Cassie couldn't clearly see where they were going, although she could make out all of the buildings on the grounds that dimly shone under the harvest moon.

She headed for the next visible building, another large confinement house, figuring that if nothing else, continually circling buildings would prevent the mystery car from catching up to them.

Mindful to keep control of the car this time, she tried to slow just a little as she approached the edge of the building and to take the corner more tightly.

Cassie misjudged.

The Civic caromed off the corner of the building in a shower of sparks, wedging a margin of the metal siding into the car's grill.

She tried to regain control, but couldn't.

With an eardrum-piercing screech, the car peeled the siding off one entire outer wall.

Despite the fact the mystery car was now mere yards behind them, Cassie slammed on her brakes.

The car hit the Civic's rear with terrific force, flinging Cassie and Missy to and fro like dolls.

The car backed up, its motor gunning, preparing to smash

into them again.

In the side mirror, Cassie saw the driver's hand reaching out of the mystery car. The hand was gripping a pistol.

Cassie jammed the gearshift into Reverse and backed up as fast as she could.

In the process, the siding was freed from the Civic's grill.

She plowed into the front of the mystery car; the gun sailed out of the mystery hand.

Shifting quickly into first, she sped ahead, even as a bizarre scene began unfolding behind them.

A tiny stampede.

Piglets-- first tens, then hundreds-- swarmed out of the opened corner of the building. In unison the piglets-- their panicked procession punctuated by the occasional lumbering sow -- cried shrilly. A song of fear, or perhaps of joyous freedom.

Whoever was in the mystery car had gotten out, and now was stepping carefully between the piglets whizzing past and around him, struggling to retrieve his dropped gun.

"Excellent job, girlfriend! Now put miles between us!" shouted Missy as Cassie took another corner... another... another... gaining speed, feeling full and sharp and alive.

"I have to find the way out of here!" Cassie cried, leaning forward in the seat, peering through the front windshield into the darkness, shifting into third, fourth...

Ahead lay what appeared to be a large area of wet asphalt. Not knowing exactly where she was in the PNI complex, or where she should go, she made the split-second decision to forge ahead.

She'd just shifted into fifth when realization draped across her shoulders like a shroud.

It wasn't a large patch of wet asphalt. It was...

"Shhhhhhiiiiiii... !"

The Civic hit the bank of dirt surrounding the waste lagoon and launched into the air.

As they sailed into the night, a fugitive moment found Cassie mesmerized by the grinning harvest moon toward which the Civic was pointing.

Missy remained silent, holding on.

Their ascent was brief.

The Civic rotated until its nose was aimed downward, like a plane coming in for a landing.

The jolt of the enormous splash shook every bone in Cassie's body.

The Civic listed left and right in the waste lagoon, tipping toward the driver's side of the car. Rancid stench and thick gurgling sounds surrounded them.

"Isn't that the way the world goes," Missy said. "Try to do a good deed and you find yourself swimming in--"

"He's coming!"

The headlights of the mystery car were visible again. Whoever it was had seen the launch and was coming to collect his prize.

The car floated to one side of the lagoon, until Missy's door was only a foot from the bank.

A headless torso suddenly appeared on the lagoon's surface and lazily rolled onto the hood of the sinking car.

"Go!" Cassie shouted, eyes wide, grabbing Missy's shoulder and shoving her. "Get out! Go and get help. If anyone can give our pursuer the slip, it's you."

A somber expression on her face, Missy opened her door against the rising tide of manure, glanced briefly at the body on the hood, then leapt gracefully to the bank.

"Godspeed!" Missy said as she sprinted away, disappearing into the autumn gloom.

Cassie released a grateful sigh when she felt the Civic's tires hit the angled bottom of the lagoon. At least she wouldn't be drowning here.

On the hood, the corpse turned over, as if searching for a more comfortable position.

Cassie sat back and tried her best to relax, fixing her gaze on the flaxen moon. She had nothing to do but wait, she decided. Perhaps like Job she needed only to trust that whatever happened, it served some higher purpose, even if it looked-- and smelled-- like torture.

Footsteps approached. Turning to look through the passenger window, she could see mere inches above ground level. But she saw a pair of work shoes there-- Size 13 EEE, if she wasn't mistaken.

One of his sweat socks had fallen, leaving an ankle exposed. Trembling fingers reached down and scratched a pattern of weeping sores there.

"Get out!"

Cassie clambered across the passenger seat and took a step deep into the manure, then another onto dry land.

Rudy Rassendeal stood there grinning, aiming his pistol at her chest.

"What do you want, Rudy?"

He started to speak, but then convulsed with a series of phlegmy coughs. He took a deep breath and pushed out an accordian wheeze. His eyes were half-lidded and rheumy, as if he was sleepy. Or insane.

"Get going!" Rudy said, stepping behind her and poking her in the small of her back with the gun's barrel. "March!"

Cassie did as she was told, walking straight toward a large Morton building a hundred yards ahead.

The happy or terrified squeals of the escaped piglets echoed in the night and were joined by a growing cacophony of other sounds: the low mournful howls of lonely coyotes; the busybody honks of a flock of geese passing overhead; the fragile chirps of crickets and cicadas, vainly resisting the death of autumn.

The wind rose and seemed to moan.

Cassie looked down at her watch. Midnight. Wasn't this when the ghosts of the Pawsitee Indians were supposed to appear? She could only hope.

When she reached the large building, Rudy shoved her with the gun barrel and she slammed against the door.

"Open it," Rudy said, voice dissolving into another round of violent coughs.

It took all of her strength for Cassie to slide open the door, but she did.

And found herself facing a gaping, hungry maw.

The monstrous barrel of the Aludium Q36 Pumpkin Modulator.

A voice from within the building called, "Happy Halloween."

13

OH, BROTHER!

Dorothy Cannell

It was like standing inside a science-fiction movie facing down the monster who had just devoured hundreds of screaming people and was eager to exert his final domination over the last few morsels of humanity left on Earth. And then the unseen voice and the man came together.

"Carl! If you aren't a treat for the eyes!" Cassie said, letting rip a laugh, the first real belly one she'd had since Ron's head had come bouncing down her stairs without so much as an apology for dropping in unannounced. Wearing ill-fitting blue jeans below his uniform shirt, Carl looked disheveled. He had always fallen mighty short when it came to brains, but his was still the long arm of the law in these parts. And such being the case, he could surely be expected to realize she wasn't that sort of woman-- the kind to lead Rudy to assume she would enjoy having a gun jabbed in her back while being escorted into lonely buildings in the dead of night.

"That's one mighty big weapon you've got there," she said, pointing an arrow-straight finger at the Modulator. "Don't suppose you're attempting to compensate for any male shortcomings, Carl!"

"Cut the social chit chat!" Rudy clearly wasn't practicing

what he'd learned in charm school as he prodded her into the shadows cast by the vast machine. But to be fair, those sores on his ankle probably made him crotchety.

"Try getting it through your pretty head, Cassie, this guy ain't no straight shooter."

"That's okay, he doesn't have to hit you square in the forehead. Any vital body part will do, just so long as there's buckets of blood and enough pain to get you screaming real good."

Cassie'd spoken lightly, but she wasn't a seasoned private eye for nothing. It had just become a textbook case of a bad day on the job. To make matters worse, Carl was just standing there, as if waiting in line for his bag of popcorn during intermission at a drive-in theater. And then it hit her, with all the force of another darned pumpkin being fired at close range from the Modulator.

She wasn't looking at one of the good guys.

And she'd thought *he* was dumb! Why hadn't she realized that sloppy police work wasn't the reason for his lackadaisical approach to solving the murders? The answer wasn't hard to find. She had been blinded by relief that she hadn't been hauled down to the station. And refused bathroom privileges for 36 hours straight, until she confessed to killing Ron and adding insult to injury by playing basketball with his head. But that was no excuse.

Women in her line of business weren't supposed to let feelings get in the way of cracking the big case. The female P.I. had to think tough, talk rough, and sleep in the buff so she could leap out of bed in the early hours of a cold hard night unencumbered by the need to shed her no-nonsense pajamas before heading out to prowl in the mean streets in unflinching pursuit of evil. A hard-nosed, single-minded existence. No steady love interest to bog her down, no children, no pets, not so much as a lone house plant demanding to be watered once or twice a year. Boy, had she blown every rule in the manual getting engaged to Ron Rassendeal, a man with two too many brothers, to add to his other iniquities. But enough of the pity party. There was no point in crying-- make that *dying*-- over spilt... blood. Time to mentally put on her trench coat, turn up her collar and look as cool as an ice-cold beer.

"I can't say as I really blame you, Carl." The sneer felt good on her face. "You have to make a better crook than you ever did a cop. Still, I hope you've gotten it in writing from Rudy here, about your pay-off, I mean. Look, don't take this the wrong way, but perhaps you should talk to a lawyer. I'd suggest Alaric Ostrogoth, but I guess that might present a conflict of interest for him, seeing as he'll be handling my inheritance from Ron. Me, running Porklips Now, Inc.! Can you believe that? Well, darn it all, neither can I! Seems to me I just won't have the time to deal with all that manure! I'll be forced to bite the bullet and shut down operations. And-- sorry to have to spoil the mood, guys-- adding me to your list of victims isn't going to help you out financially. After Alaric phoned with the news, I went down to his office and made out my own will, leaving the land to the Peoria Park District."

The lie came out as slick as a newborn pig. And why wouldn't they believe her? They had no way of knowing Alaric had only phoned her tonight.

Carl's expression didn't falter. It had always taken him longer to digest the smallest piece of information than the average person would have needed to read the Bible cover to cover. But Rudy was certainly taken aback. In fact, he took a good two or three steps away from her. And being a person who had always take time out to smell the flowers, she savored the relief of not having his gun directly on her back.

"Hey, you've got it all wrong, Cassie!" Rudy sounded deeply hurt. "I'm not in with this slime bag and his lot. I've been keeping an eye on him for days, and when I followed him out here tonight, I guessed he was taking me to where they'd been hiding the Modulator."

"You believe that cock and bull?" Carl leaned against the Modulator. The obvious attempt to look nonchalant looked ridiculous as Carl was dwarfed by its size. "Makes a lot of sense, don't it? Him pointing that gun at you, not me."

"The creep's got a point," Cassie said, looking over her shoulder at Rudy.

"I was agitated is all; my hand was shaking. And I guess I used your back without thinking... to steady it. No..." his sigh seemed to blow through the building like a full-scale wind. "I'm lying to you."

"Told you so." Carl managed to sound like a Boy Scout.

Rudy ignored him. "The truth is, I'm a coward, always have been. What I was doing, Cassie, was using you for a human shield. I reckoned that if there was anything of the cop left in Carl, he'd think twice before shooting a woman. And here I was, hoping I could start over. Do as Reverend Roylott is always suggesting. Put aside childish things, like greed, sloth, lust and fornication, and take on what goes along with being a man."

Swept up in a tide of emotion, Rudy took another couple of steps backward, brushed against a rough-hewn wooden bench and sat down. Head lowered. Hands dangling from limp wrists. "Can you ever forgive me, Cassie?

"We'll discuss that, after you tell me what you know."

"I'm a man in need of special sympathy," he pleaded. "I've got the worst case of poison ivy all around my ankles. And no cream I've used has helped."

"Let's hope that's all it is." Cassie was about to elaborate, but Carl, understandably feeling left out, interrupted.

"But I want to talk about how the Modulator works," put in Carl plaintively. "It's really amazing."

Unasked, he began lecturing.

"This monster here, the Aludium Q36 Pumpkin Modulator, gets its name from a similar device, the Illudium Pew-36 Explosive Space Modulator, a planet-destroying raygun owned by Marvin The Martian in some Bugs Bunny cartoons.

"But this Modulator," Carl continued, "was built to compete in the annual world punkin' chunkin' contest held at Lewes, Del. Just for fun. Using compressed air, it's hurled pumpkins more than 2,700 feet-- a world record-- via a 100-foot-long barrel. It weighs 18 tons. A control panel..."

Cassie recognized the ploy for what it was, an attempt to bore her and Rudy into deep sleep, so he could dispose of them without worrying about resistance-- or gunfire from Rudy. And despite his lack of a complete uniform, Carl might be armed. "Men and machinery!"

Giving a creditable chuckle, Cassie shook her head. "It's something we women just can't figure, so if you won't think me rude, I'd like to hear what Rudy has to say."

"There was always sibling rivalry between all of us," he said. "Ron... Rhiney... Our parents encouraged it. 'You've got to learn to grind each other under foot before you take on the world' was their motto. And it worked! Even though they split with Rhiney, I know that deep in their hearts they thought he, like Ron and me, had grown into the sort of blood-sucking, dog-eat-dog men any mom and dad could rightly be proud of. But when Ron died, I started looking at things different. He'd lost you, Cassie, because of his business dealings. And then to lose his head... it put the wind up me, it did. Suddenly I found myself having second thoughts about the casino. Was it right, morally speaking, to use the Indian thing?

"And what if," he shuddered, "those spirits Red is always harping about did take up against me and rose from their burial mounds to take after me? I got so shook up I even talked to Rhiney, get him to see that maybe he was going down the wrong path. And when words did no good, I tried another way."

"You sent him Care packages," said Cassie, still keeping both eyes on Carl.

"The only living thing Rhiney ever gave a damn about was that pig." Rudy's head sank lower. "He'd lost Bonita a while ago to a succession of lovers, because of his lousy neglect."

"That's right!" The harshness of Carl's voice might have made Cassie jump if she hadn't already exceeded her yearly quota of feminine frailty by fainting-- whatever the physical cause-- earlier that day. "Rhiney never deserved a woman like Bonita. The most sensational, sensuous, sexy woman on the face of the Earth. I got to know her when I'd stop in at that restaurant where she worked as a waitress. And I'm just one of thousands of Real Men who would have married her at the drop of a hat."

"Or your pants," Rudy said, looking up to glare at him.

"You're in love with her, too." It wouldn't have needed a P.I. to make that deduction.

"Maybe... I guess so," Rudy said. "Sorry, Cassie."

"I'll get by" was her dry response. "One of the reasons I

didn't marry your late brother is that the name Rassendeal sounds, all too suitably, like some sort of foreign word for a shady operation. And for all your proclaimed change of heart, I wouldn't share a credit history, let alone a bed, with you for all the pumpkins in Morton, or marigolds in Pekin. You get the idea"

Outside the building, the wind picked up, moaning and groaning in an impatient sort of way, as if it too were eager to have all the answers. Cassie was swept up into the dislocated feeling that she was trapped in one of those round robins, where a bunch of writers all write a chapter of the same book and try to have it come out making brilliant sense. This got her thinking about Morris the Explainer, the man who'd told her he wrote the endings to mystery novels for authors who discovered on reaching the final chapter that they couldn't sort out all the clues and red herrings they'd scattered willy-nilly throughout their manuscripts. He had told her that, among other things. Just as a number of people had told her a bunch of other stuff that for the most part she had swallowed whole without first tearing it apart, shred by shred, before even starting to chew on it like a dog with a bone. Shame almost swamped her. She was a disgrace to a revered profession. She should be stripped of her P.I. license before being thrust naked as the White White Witch into the world. It didn't do any good to tell herself that the best in the business might have been thrown off track by so many of the suspects having names beginning with 'R.' As her mother used to say when handing around the gravy boat-- "You take your lumps and eat them."

"Tell me more about Bonita," she urged Carl. But he didn't get to respond, because even as a glow, rivaling the sunrises Red loved so much, spread over his dimwitted face, the woman in question entered the building. A vision to behold even in her faded print dress and her hair pulled back into a pioneer woman's knot. Her impact was palpable. Even Cassie felt her raw power. Here was one who had simmered on a slow burner too long in an empty marriage before finally reaching the boiling point of red-hot womanhood. What man could resist the slow swing of her broad hips or the slumberous passion in her dark eyes? Certainly not the two men present. Rudy dropped his gun and had to scramble to retrieve it, while Carl looked through him as if he were an open doorway, oblivious to everything and anything but Bonita.

"I knew I'd find you here." Bonita's lush lips curved into a tender smile as she advanced toward him, stepping over Rudy's hand and brushing Cassie with her skirt. "My dear, brave, exquisitely proportioned angel love!"

"I-- I had to come," Carl mumbled, trembling like a schoolboy. "I had to wipe the Modulator for fingerprints. And I didn't mind that it would take hours-- perhaps days. Red got away when I tried to arrest him. And I knew what was going to happen. I'd be branded a bungler and someone else would be put on the case. Someone really wanting to solve it."

"I know! I know! My turtle dove!" Bonita drew him to her opulent bosom. "You've been so wonderful! Taking care of those nasty murders for me. The only one I felt sorry about," turning to half face Rudy and Cassie, "was Sam Sheafhecker. The innocent boy, so diligent in his detective duties, returned. He stayed to spend the night. And he said he'd heard me talking in my sleep. Somehow, that made me feel real cheap," a sob broke her voice apart, "murdering the guy on our very first date. Not that I had to do it myself."

"And you never will while there's breath in my body," Carl

glowered over her shoulder at the two onlookers of this misty-eyed scene. "I don't know why you won't let me get rid of Rhiney for you. That way we could get married, Bonnie, make it all nice and legal."

"This is breaking my heart," said Cassie.

"Mine, too," Rudy said, sounding as though he meant it. "Honest, Bonita, I had no idea you had anything to do with the murders. I got suspicious of Carl on account of the way he was handling, or should I say *not* handling, the case. Even he can only carry stupidity so far. What I wasn't able to figure out was the motive."

"Love!" Bonita breathed fire into the word. "His for me, and..."

"And yours for half the male population of Illinois," Cassie inquired tartly. "Just how many goons do you have trapped in your homicidal spell?"

"You're mad because I pretended to be your friend, to throw you off my trail." Bonita let go of Carl and swung around to look her full in the eyes. "And I can't say as I blame you after that pumpkin head business. That was Paisano's idea. He can be such a sadist at times. Just this afternoon he toyed with that reporter Maggie Lynch, pretending we were going to give her an exclusive, while all the time he was getting ready to kill her. At first I thought he was right. She's the sort to keep poking around until she got at the truth. But, finally, I was unconvinced and had Paisano release her.

"He pouted some, but I sent him back to Toluca to make pasta," she continued. "Cooking makes him feel so manly."

"And as much as I adore all the men in my life, one of them," she turned back to pinch Carl's cheek, "one of them might have cracked under the pressure and given the game away."

"You sure don't pick 'em for their brains," agreed Cassie. "Two of them certainly talk too much: Morris the Explainer and Jose O'Shea. They told me Morris was in the Witness Protection program, something only an idiot would let slip, let alone tell flat out to a total stranger."

"They do tend to get a bit carried away," Bonita smiled fondly, "but they were so darling about dropping everything to tail you to Springfield. So it wouldn't be nice of me to nit-pick that instead of keeping behind your car, they got to shooting the breeze and ended up at the rest stop ahead of you. Sure, I would rather they had kept a low profile when you walked in. But given Jose's looks, that's never easy. And dear Morris can't resist an audience for one of his stories. His heart was in the right place. He really hoped he'd spun you a tale that would muddle your thinking to the point where you wouldn't be able to untangle it ever again."

Cassie wasn't about to admit he'd come close to succeeding. This was only partly due to embarrassment. She couldn't afford to waste words. The tension mounted with every passing second. Carl, and Rudy with his gun back in his hand, might have been a couple of statues left stored in the building along with the Modulator. All expression had been wiped off their faces as with a damp sponge.

"You said Paisano wanted to kill Maggie Lynch," she said.

"And I wouldn't go for it," Bonita both looked and sounded noble. "It was the same as when Carl here asked-- begged me-- to let him do away with Rhiney. I just couldn't bring myself. He's not something I should ever have dragged home to Mother, but so long as he's never home I can live with him. Maggie isn't the threat that Sam was, and having him killed upset me real bad. With Ron and Mux it was different..."

"You're responsible for Mux's death?" Cassie asked.

"Who else?"

"Just stating the obvious." Cassie allowed herself a flicker of relief. She had been right when it occurred to her that Missy had lied about killing him. She was a woman who carried attention-seeking to new highs. Very few females-- even women whose families and heritage were disrespected, even women victimized by assaults-- would have reacted to being ditched by a man she hardly knew the way she had done. Cassie could have understood Missy's outrage at discovering Rice was a cross-dresser if he'd snuck out in one of her sweaters and stretched it irretrievably out of shape. And, yes, it was irksome to remember the times he had harped from the pulpit about the evils of women wearing slacks. But such was life. And Missy, having ridden with the motorcycle boys, hadn't led a particularly sheltered life. Still, Cassie couldn't help but like her, wacky or not, and be glad she didn't have to risk their budding friendship by putting in a report to the authorities.

"One of Paisano's thugs, a guy in war paint, killed Mux," Bonita was now saying. "And I wasn't real happy he dressed up like a Native American and used an arrow that would point suspicion at your partner. Because that's what all this had been about for me. Trying to restore the land to those of us that love and respect it. And if the only way to do that was to murder them that were out to pollute and destroy it, then I was the girl! Isn't it bad enough that people who've never been there talk down Peoria like it's some sort of joke? And, even worse, they don't know the small towns here about even exist! They think because we don't have mountains or a sea shore that we don't have scenery. To most people Illinois is Chicago. Well, I could tell them! There's nothing like the view I get from my house. Not just in summer when the corn's up. But also in winter when there's nothing but sky. When I realized how life was going to be with Rhiney, I thought about walking out, but it was too late. My roots were already in deep in the soil, my soul in the storm clouds of spring, my life in all the living things growing.

"They're taking the 'heart' out of the 'heartland'," she said, her voice cracking. "And no one was going to take that from me. Like I said, it was all for love."

"You sure are something, Bonita," Carl finally spoke.

"Save the compliments, angel cake. I'm not in the mood." She sounded sad and tired, and looked like what she was, that most disappointing of life's creations, an idealist gone badly wrong.

"If I'd only myself to think about, I'd turn myself in," she said. "But I can't do that to you, Carl, or the other guys. It wouldn't be decent. So, I'll close my eyes, while you kill Cassie."

"You're forgetting Rudy," pointed out the intended victim.

"No, I'm not," Bonita's smile didn't quite reach her eyes. "Take a look at him! He's realized that he'd rather be on the side of the bad girls than the good guys any day of the week."

With a sinking heart, Cassie decided she was right, then saw Rudy shake his head.

"I can't do that, Bonnie," he said in a voice thick with regret, "but I promise I'll visit you often in jail and bring you presents of lingerie from Victoria's Secret. I expect you'd even get to wear it if I picked something in orange."

Rudy wasn't looking at Carl, who'd picked up a manure-encrusted pitch fork, leveled it, and advanced toward them.

But Cassie saw. She was the woman who'd picked up a

pitcher and hurled it at Ron Rassendeal, putting a dent in his nose and an end to their relationship. Now she ducked down, grabbed at the bench Rudy had sat on, and sent it skidding across the floor to hit Carl with brutal force in the shins. Giving vent to a blood-curdling yelp, he dropped his barnyard weapon. And as Rudy reacted, kicking it away and pointing his pistol at them, Cassie glanced once more at the Modulator before smiling at Bonita.

"Sometimes the less complicated the better," she said. "And sometimes, whatever Rice Roylott may think, judgment is not deferred."

Epilogue
ALL SAINTS'
DAY EVE

"So, let me get this straight," said Maggie, taking a swig from a Sam Adams cherry wheat beer before returning to her reporter's notebook. "Bonita became a sort of eco-terrorist?"

Missy giggled and slightly turned her espresso, in a tiny white cup. Morning traffic and Bradley students briskly moved along Main outside One World Coffee's big plate-glass windows.

Cassie nodded and said, "Yeah. She was frustrated by love-- and a state legislature that can't find its bottom with both hands. So she got some of her men to help her get back at Ron for the mega-hog farm and Mux for the do-nothing General Assembly."

"That's redundant," said Maggie, laughing. "But wait. 'Get back,' you said? Hmm." She tapped the table with her pen.

"'Revenge' overpowered the area," Cassie said. "In Mux's killing, one of Bonita's zombies used a 'Revenge' flyer he'd found. Impulse. Or sowing confusion. But some are getting over a thirst for revenge. Rudy's talking to authorities. I'm still a little weak, but I feel better about myself. How about you Missy?"

"Oh, I'm better," she said softly. "When I fled the wreck, I ran and ran and finally felt cleansed somehow. All the rides, the lies-- sorry, again, Cas'-- the fear and anger were gone by the time I got back with a State trooper, and it was all over."

Looking at her watch, Maggie said, "I've got a deadline if this goes out today. Broadcast just has headlines; I need details. Who killed your boyfriend, Cassie? Who used the Modulator?"

Cassie's mind drifted off to late last night, after Red finally found her at home, reading her Bible. She'd said, "Psalm 91, Red: '...You will not fear the terror of the night, nor the arrow that flies by day, nor the pestilence that stalks in darkness, nor the destruction that wastes at noonday'."

"That's nice," he'd said, smiling, relieved to see her alive. "I prefer, 'Pray for what you want; work for what you need'."

"Potawatomie prayer?"

"Fortune cookie."

Maggie's bark interrupted her reverie. "Earth to Cassie!"

"Oh, sorry. It looks like Paisano or one of his dim bulbs got Bonita's order to kill Ron. Later-- after my partner showed a peculiar peccadillo by mutilating the corpse, before he tossed Rudy into the lagoon-- Bonita and Carl went back to dispose of the evidence and thought they'd fling Ron into the manure-- head first. They used the Modulator, gave up when the head went awry, and just tossed the rest of Ron's body in the drink."

"Drink? You mean, crap," Maggie said. "So this Tazewell cop ended up moving the Modulator around to hide it, huh? Jeez. Say, are you OK, Cassie? How's your health?"

"When I spoke to Ostrogoth this morning about closing PNI, he set me up with a doctor," Cassie said, sipping an indulgence, a cappuccino. "I called; the doc said pfiesteria is serious. I'm going in at 1. I feel like a lab rat."

"I feel great! Sorry," Missy said, blushing a bit. "It's just that there's a weight off me. I'm looking forward to celebrating all the holidays. Casmir Pulaski Day is only a few months off!"

Cassie looked at a newspaper nearby. Opinion polls about next week's election showed Mux, though dead, was still ahead.

•

Cassie hadn't left with the other women. She wanted, needed, to sit and sip her drink. A man approached at her elbow, a man with a look that would have told her, even if he hadn't been holding a notepad and pencil, that he was a reporter.

"I hate to bother you," he said with the blatant insincerity of the breed, "but I just happened to catch sight of you from across the room and wondered if I could ask you a few questions about the murders."

"Sorry." Cassie could lie, too. "I'm waiting for someone."

"Well, at least let me make sure I spell your name right."

"C-A-N-I-N-E."

"And that's pronounced..."

"Just as you'd expect," Cassie was surprised to hear herself say, seeing a shadow at the door. "Oh, there's my friend now."

And in a manner of speaking, this was the truth, because it was the Rev. Rice Roylott coming toward her.

"How about I buy you both a drink?" Having taken the time to grow a thick skin, the newsman wasn't about to shed it lightly. But when Cassie stood and balled her fists, he left.

"Who was that?" asked Rice, sitting down.

"The press."

"Cassie... Cassie, I could take you away from all that."

What did he think he was, Calgon? She barely avoided voicing this thought. At least for now, the Porklips case-- as she'd always think of it-- had made her a kinder, gentler woman.

"You know how I feel about you," Rice continued, his voice wheedling. "My love for you has been both my shame and my pride. But now I'm a free man. We can finally make a life together, build a home, raise a family that's different than the one I came from. You see, there's something even you haven't figured out. My full name is Rice Roylott Rassendeal; I'm Rudy's or Rhiney's or maybe Ron's twin. Our mother was a bit vague about such things. Too many children, too little time."

This was some twist, thought Cassie wryly. The good instead of the evil twin.

"It might have helped with the confusion if your parents had ventured on to a new letter of the alphabet," she suggested. "What happened? Were you disowned like Rhiney?"

"It was the other way around," Rice said, leaning forward on his elbows. "I asked to be sent to live with relatives when I was three and the others kept switching the radio to rock 'n' roll when I wanted to hear the word of the Lord-- on the air."

"Good for you, Rice," Cassie said, placing her hand on his. "But you've got to understand that you and I can never have an intimate relationship. I'm a P.I., married to the job of outsmarting bad guys-- and girls. Thanks to your brother Ron, I now know there's no room in my life for commitment. I've cancelled my subscription to *Readers' Digest* and I shall never watch another mini-series on TV. So when it comes to men..."

Her voice broke off because another shadow had momentarily filled the doorway. And now it was Red coming toward her. His face still seemed as creased with worry as his work clothes. He wasn't a man to turn many female heads, but Cassie felt hers swim as she left Rice sitting at the table and crossed the room to her once-and-future partner, one slow, purposeful step at a time, because there was no need to rush. And, being a woman, Cassie Canine had all the patience of Job.

Contributors

NANCY ATHERTON is the author of the Aunt Dimity mystery series (**Aunt Dimity's Death, Aunt Dimity and The Duke** and **Aunt Dimity's Good Deed**). Featuring the sleuth-from-beyond, the books have become favorites with readers seeking pure and simple domestic escape. Aunt Dimity's world, which author Dorothy Cannell describes as "a kind, gentle place where oatmeal cookies, stuffed bunnies, and cozy cottages bring warmth and joy into the heart of every reader," continues to grow this year with **Aunt Dimity Digs In**, scheduled to be published by Viking/Penguin in March.

Nancy lives next door to a cornfield in central Illinois.

TERRY BIBO of the Peoria **Journal Star** has been cited as the top columnist in Illinois by both the Associated Press and the Illinois Press Association. In more than 20 years with the paper, she's covered everything from obituaries to Peoria's City Hall. As an editor, she was project director for the **Journal**'s award-winning "Leadership Challenge" series, and published **The Rest of Baker's Best** and **Mary, Me** for her late husband, Rick Baker. She lives in Elmwood with her husband, Bill Knight; their son, Rusty Baker; five cats; one dog; and numerous Shetland pony-sized dustballs.

An avid hiker, Eagle Scout, founder of a successful mutual fund, and winner of the Mathematics and Science Award from Rensselaer Polytechnic Institute, STEVEN BURGAUER lives in Peoria with his family. He has written extensively in the fields of investment management, finance and economics. In addition, Burgauer has written four science fiction titles, his most recent

Dorothy Cannell

being **In The Shadow of Omen**. A short story of his has appeared in the **Eureka Literary Magazine**. Burgauer's work has been mentioned in both **Locus** and **Science Fiction Chronicle**. His most recent book has been reviewed in **Prometheus**, the journal of the Libertarian Futurist Society, which also has nominated him for its 1997 science fiction award.

DOROTHY CANNELL was born in Nottingham, England, and has lived in Peoria since 1965 with her husband and four children. The author of the popular Ellie Haskell series of mysteries-- including **God Save The Queen, How To Murder The Man of Your Dreams, Femmes Fatal, Down The Garden Path** and others-- Cannell launched her successful career selling a short story after taking a writing course at Illinois Central College. Her first novel, **The Thin Woman** (1984), was named Best Paperback Novel of The Year by the Romance Writers of America. Her **Widows Club** (1988) earned nominations for both an Agatha Award and an Anthony Award.

DAVID EVERSON is the author of six mystery novels and two short stories featuring downstate Illinois gumshoes Robert Miles and Mitch Norris, Midcontinential Op and Associate, whose special area of expertise is the hardball work of Illinois politics. Ballantine Ivy published **Recount** (1987), **Rebound** (1988), **Rematch** (1989) and **A Capital Killing** (1990) as paperback originals. **Recount** and **Rebound** were both nominated for a Shamus Award for best paperback original by the Private Eye Writers of America. St. Martin's Press published **Suicide Squeeze** (1991) and **False Profits** (1992) in hardcover. **Suicide Squeeze** also appeared in paperback from Ivy in 1995.

Everson is currently working on a new series featuring reporters Ross Miller and Maggie Lynch, the first entry of which will be **If Men Were Angels**.

A professor of political science, Everson is currently Associate Chancellor of the University of Illinois at Springfield.

PHILIP JOSE FARMER is considered one of the great science fiction writers in history. His revolutionary impact on the genre was first felt with his Hugo Award-winning novella, **The Lovers** (1952), and reverberated through **Flesh** (1960) and the literary landmark "Riverworld" series-- starting in 1971 with the Hugo Award-winning **To Your Scattered Bodies Go**.

Critic Peter Lamborn Wilson in 1989 called Farmer "a supreme pulpster [and] more: a Trickster, a 'rough' surrealist, a progenitor of new waves, dangerous visions and cyber-porno weirdness... an ancestor, but unlike other ancestral science fiction figures, he has never become an embarrassment, a 'BOF,' a curmudgeon."

Ultimately, Wilson commented, Farmer is 'The Sage of Peoria,' that 'Holy City by the Kickapoo'."

His first story was published by **Adventure** magazine in

Nancy Atherton   **Terry Bibo**

1946. Since then, his 70-plus books range from the **Dayworld** and **World of Tiers** book series to short-story collections and pseudonymous works (by Kilgore Trout, Leo Queequeg Tincrowder, Rod Keen and other pen names). His 1967 novella **Riders of The Purple Wage** also won a Hugo Award.

Born in 1918, he was raised in Peoria, where he earned a B.A. at Bradley University in 1950. Following years of working for the aerospace industry in various cities, he and his wife Bette in 1970 returned to Peoria, where they still reside.

A mystery novel set in Peoria, **Nothing Burns in Hell**, is his newest book; his new Tarzan title is scheduled to be published later this year.

JOSEPH FLYNN is the author of the novels **Digger** and **The Concrete Inquisition**, and a screenplay, **Comrades**, optioned by 20th Century Fox. He lives in Springfield, where he's working on his next novel.

JULIE KISTLER is well-known among fans of romantic comedy for her fast-paced, light-hearted romps. Kistler's 15th book, **Fantasy Wife**, was a Waldenbooks Bestseller for

Harlequin American Romance. **Black Jack Brogan**, one of her most popular titles, was a finalist for Romance Writers of America's prestigious RITA Award. **Touch Me Not** (1997) and **Tuesday's Knight** (1998) are her latest works.

A former lawyer, Kistler is a frequent speaker at conferences and workshops, on topics ranging from legal issues to laughter. She acted as a member of the Romance Writers of America Board of Directors and received the RWA service award in 1994. This year she will serve as President-elect of Novelists, Inc., a professional organization for writers of popular fiction. Kistler is scheduled to be President in 1999, for NINC's 10th anniversary.

Also resident drama critic for the Champaign **News-Gazette**, Kistler is a Peoria native with numerous ties to central Illinois. She is also a big fan of "March Madness" at the Peoria Civic Center. She and her husband live in Bloomington with their cat Thisbe, their computers, and a large collection of books on movies, theater, history and sports.

JERRY KLEIN is the dean of central Illinois feature

Jerry Klein

Philip Jose Farmer

David Everson

writers. A longtime editorial writer, columnist and critic with the Peoria **Journal Star**, Klein's writings also have appeared in the **New York Times, Reader's Digest, Redbook** and other periodicals.

His books include the novel **Fathersday**, the history titles **Peoria!, A Century of Music** and **Peoria Industry: A Pictorial History**, and nonfiction works such as **Played in Peoria** and **Lusts of The Prairie Preachers** (with Jack Bradley). The native Peorian still writes a Sunday column for the **Journal Star** and a weekly column for the **Metamora Herald**. He and his wife

Julie Kistler

Steven Burgauer

Joel Steinfeldt

Mary live in the countryside outside Germantown Hills, where they raised seven children.

BILL KNIGHT is an award-winning journalist who teaches at Western Illinois University. A weekly commentator on Illinois Public Radio, he also freelances and writes columns for the **Times** newspaper group and **The Labor Paper**, both in the Peoria area.

Knight has written three books about central Illinois (**R.F.D.**, **R.F.D. Journal** and **R.F.D. Notebook**); edited **Peoria People** (1988), **The Eye of The Reporter** (1996, with Deckle McLean) and **Midwestern Gothic** (1994, by Jack Bradley); and published two collections of media criticism by Walter Brasch (**Enquiring Minds and Space Aliens** and **Sex & The Single Beer Can**). He's also written for academic titles such as **The Encyclopedia of Civil Rights** and a **Dictionary of Literary Biographies** volume. His forthcoming books include an anthology of radio features (**Fair Comment**) and a mystery novel (**Storm Front**). He, his wife Terry and their son Rusty live in Elmwood.

TRACY KNIGHT is a clinical psychologist who lives and practices in Carthage, Illinois. His short fiction in the horror, suspense, mystery and science fiction genres has appeared in numerous anthologies, including **Werewolves, Murder for Father, Whitley Strieber's Aliens, The UFO Files**, and three of the books in the "Cat Crimes" series. He contributed a chapter to the Writer's Digest book **Writing Horror**, and writes a regular column on Psychology and Crime Fiction for **Mystery Scene** magazine. He recently completed his first novel.

Bill Knight   **Tracy Knight**

Chicago native GARRY MOORE is a news anchor and producer at WEEK-TV Channel 25, Peoria's NBC affiliate. After graduating from Bradley University, Moore started reporting at WXCL-AM in Peoria, and his career in news has continued to include radio at stations such as WBGE-FM and WEEK-FM. His journalism has taken him to South Africa, the

Garry Moore   **Joseph Flynn**

Dominican Republic and across the United States, and he's done documentary work with Peoria's public TV station, WTVP-TV.

Besides broadcasting, Moore is a frequent cultural arts presenter at central Illinois schools, camps, workshops, prisons and seminars, for which he's been honored with the Imperative Award from the Pekin YWCA and induction into the Downstate African Hall of Fame Museum.

Moore also is a drummer with the Wazobia Dance Troupe, and a novelist (**The Jesus Crisis**).

He and his wife Denise live in Bloomington, and own and operate a gift shop in Normal-- where they hope to someday carry Garry's books.

Born in Springfield, JOEL STEINFELDT grew up in Ruston, La., before moving to Waukegan and eventually Pekin, where he currently resides. He began work for the Pekin **Daily Times** as a free-lance correspondent, then moved on to circulation manager, reporter, photographer, paginator, assistant city editor and, briefly, acting editor-- all before returning to his current job as city editor. This is his first literary work.